MW01232670

Sasquatch 8

The Anthology

Jeffrey B Miley

Other books by Jeffrey B Miley-

Pastor Jeff Adventure Series:
May the Peace of Christ Not Kill You
Death in The Living Waters
Love Thine Enemy Unto Death
Blood Doctrine
Nothing Is Hidden That Will Not Be Revealed
and the dead shall rise
The Eden Inferno
The Trinity Deception
Revenge In The Woods Series:
Shriek
Shriek 2-Cain's Revenge
Shriek 3-3
Shriek 4: The Chair
Shriek 5: The Witch Is Back
Sasquatch Adventures Series:
Sasquatch-The Cave
Sasquatch 2-The Mask
Sasquatch 3-The Troop
Sasquatch 4-The Clone
Sasquatch 5-The Pioneers
Sasquatch 6-The Forgotten Ozark Forest Devils
Sasquatch 7-The Slot Canyon
Sasquatch 8-The Anthology
full blood moon series:
full blood moon
full blood moon 2
full blood moon 3-Winnie's Springs
Other titles:
Killing The Past
Time Jaunt-Saving Custer
Manny
The Bouncy House
The Silver Cigar Series-Alien At My Window
The Silver Cigar Series-Aliens In My Basement

Table of Contents

The Camera

Aperture 1

The noise of the crowd filled the room. There was pleasant conversation, the clinking of wine glasses, the rings of unmuted cellphones and the intermittent sound of the artificial door chime every time someone entered or exited the gallery.

The door chime was driving Albert mad. This was a swanky affair. The invited guests were the wealthy, upper crust of Pittsburgh. Most of them resided in Squirrel Hill North, Regent Square, Fairywood or Point Breeze.

Some were from old money, and others enjoyed the windfall of high technology industry. Albert would take their money, no matter from where they hailed. It was all green. He laughed at that thought. The truth was, no one used dirty, green money any longer. They used plastic. So he resolved to say that he would take their plastic: Mastercard, Visa, American Express and even Discover.

He was observing the crowd from the studio loft. It wasn't time to make his appearance quite yet. The door chime went off once again. Damn thing was so crass in this setting. *For God's sake, this isn't some corner Korean grocery store*, he thought.

The Michaelson Gallery had been on Forbes Avenue for over forty years. It was nestled in Pittsburgh's downtown historic district. They hosted art and photography exhibits once a month. This was his first show here, and he was feeling fortunate to have been invited.

Albert had seventeen photos on display. The other photographers were already down below acting too eager. He would wait a few more minutes. He had something special to reveal.

As a nature photographer, he had a knack for capturing the raw beauty of the surrounding mountains. With the right filter, he could make the most mundane flora or fauna leap to life. It was his gift, and he was proud of it.

After a few more moments, he made his entrance. Mr. Campbell, the gallery manager, announced in a loud voice, "Ladies and gentlemen, Mr. Albert Clarion, one of our featured photographers."

Many people in the crowd quietly clapped, trying to keep their wine glasses steady so as to not spill a drop of their free wine. Clapping was the polite thing to do.

Albert had noticed the photo that drew the most attention from his earlier perch in the loft. It was a picture he had taken in Blue Knob State Park. The subject was a beautiful stand of striped maples. The filter he employed made the bark more pronounced and exotic.

But the hidden surprise, or what some people called the Easter egg in the photo, was to the left of the group of trees. For him it had gone unnoticed for weeks, until he had a print blown up for the gallery showing.

Even then, Albert didn't see it. It was his little neighbor boy who would come and visit him from time to time. Joey Porter was seven years old and filled with curiosity that sometimes drove Albert nuts.

He was being raised by his single mother, whom Albert had slept with three times, so far. The kid was smart, polite and cute. And since Albert didn't have the most active of social lives, he let the kid hang with him from time to time.

It was during one of those times that Joey asked, "Who is the guy standing in the background?"

There was no one there that day. Albert asked Joey to show him what he saw, so Joey did. Albert was shocked. He set the photo under his lighted magnifying ring.

After staring at the image for over three minutes, he grabbed a ruler and took some measurements. He did some quick math, based on distance and perspective.

It didn't look quite human. He could discern no clothing, but rather what appeared to be hair from head to foot. And if his calculations were right, the thing stood eight feet tall. Up to now, he had just seen it as another tree, off to the left and in the background. Only after Joey identified it as possibly a man standing in the picture did it become apparent to Albert. And now Albert couldn't un-see it.

As the people in the gallery were milling about and looking at the photos, the striped maples seem to be the most popular photos. He wondered what the onlookers were seeing in his photo. Did they see some guy in the background? Or were they like Albert, and they didn't see it at all?

It was time to become the master of his own destiny. He stood in front of the popular photo.

"Ladies and gentlemen," he began. "May I have your attention?"

Mr. Campbell became nervous and angry. The participants in gallery shows were not supposed to grandstand. These gallery events were not carnival sideshows. The exhibits were to speak for themselves. The artists were not to speak at all, unless engaged by the guests.

Albert continued, "As I have observed you here tonight, this photo seems to have garnered the most interest. I am curious as to why. What did you see that drew your attention? Was it the beautiful linear qualities of the striped maples brought to life or something else?"

Campbell waited to see where this was going. This most assuredly would be Albert Clarion's last showing at this gallery.

An older, very distinguished looking gentleman spoke up, "I am curious as to why you incorporated the man to the left. He is almost non-descript, yet he is there."

A woman spoke up, "I don't think it is a man. It looks like it isn't wearing clothing. It is all one color."

Albert was excited as he heard the crowd murmuring. Several guests stepped forward to see what they didn't see before. Campbell found himself intrigued by the crowd's reaction. He wondered if Clarion was possibly a marketing genius.

The crowd was absorbed in sidebar discussions as to whether the figure was a man or something else. And some were trying to ascribe the presence of the figure as having a deeper meaning.

Albert Clarion and Mr. Campbell both watched the assemblage for a few moments. Campbell wanted to see where this was headed, and how it might benefit the gallery, if at all. Albert wanted to choose the best time for his reveal.

"Ladies and gentlemen," Albert began, "allow me to explain the mystery and replace it with another. When I took the photo, I did not see the figure. It was pointed out to me by a seven-year-old boy. I have an enlarged section of the figure, and I'll tell you my guess as to what it is."

He walked over to an oversized valise that had been zippered and leaning against the wall. As the guests watched intently, he withdrew the enlarged section of the photo. The only enhancement was a bit of sharpening for detail's sake.

He placed the enlarged print on an empty easel beside the original entry. Every eye was upon the new piece of evidence.

Finally, a distinguished, tuxedo-clad, old codger said, "So what is your guess, Mr. Clarion? What are we looking at?"

"This photo was taken at Blue Knob State Park, and that my friends is the creature known as Big Blue," Clarion announced.

The crowd's murmur reached a new crescendo. Some had heard of Big Blue and some had not. It was Mr.

Campbell who asked, "For clarification sake, Mr. Clarion, who or what is Big Blue?"

"It is a what, to be most precise. That, my esteemed patrons of the arts, is the sasquatch that has been sighted for years in the park. Actually, sightings began in 1952 when the Claysburg Air Force Station began operations there before it became a park," Albert informed them.

The buzz was reaching a crescendo and Albert couldn't have been happier. Good fortune had finally smiled upon him.

"Why should we believe you?" asked a curvaceous young woman with long, straight, brunette hair. She looked like new money, considering the barbed wire tattoo wrapping around her left ankle and the large hoop earrings dangling from her ears. Old money, even in their youth, usually looked much more conservative.

"I have no reason to lie," Albert said. "I only seek to share my accidental good fortune."

"I'll give you five thousand for the original," said a nerdy looking computer geek. He was definitely a tech millionaire, as far as Albert could tell.

"Ten thousand!" came another offer.

Albert was stunned. He would have jumped at one thousand dollars.

Mr. Campbell, seeing an opportunity and wanting the gallery to benefit from the ten percent commission arrangement, spoke up, "Ladies and gentlemen, let's keep this orderly, please."

He then took over as auctioneer, "We have a bid of ten thousand, anyone else?"

"Twenty!"

"Twenty-five!"

"Forty thousand!"

When the bidding ended, the old, distinguished-looking man whom had asked the first question, regarding the composition including the figure in the background, won the bidding war.

Ninety-five thousand dollars.

Albert felt lightheaded. This was way beyond what he could have ever imagined.

One would think this day couldn't possibly get stranger than what had already transpired, but it did.

After Albert had signed the waivers, released his photo for sale and received his money, he chose to sit quietly by himself. He watched as the exhibit wound down and the patrons filed out of the gallery, one well-heeled couple following the next. And he heard that chintzy door chime announcing each exit.

A short, round, young man with a million-dollar redhead on his arm approached him.

"The name is Jamie Booth. I'm the creator of Fortress Attack. You probably heard of the game if you haven't heard of me." Booth waited for a response.

Albert stood up and said, "Yessir. I play your game on-line with friends. Great game. What may I do for you?"

"Get me a detailed portrait of Big Blue, with proof it is legitimate, and I'll buy it from you for five hundred thousand dollars. If you can physically capture Big Blue, I'll give you a million dollars."

Albert felt lightheaded for the second time on this day.

Booth held out his hand, to seal the deal.

Albert did not shake it. First, he needed to tell the man something, "Mr. Booth, I can't guarantee anything. Sasquatch hunters have been looking for Big Blue for decades, with nothing but a few indistinct casts of footprints to show for their efforts."

"Are you not interested in my money?" Booth asked.

Albert shook his hand and said, "I'll do my best."

Aperture 2

Albert sat at his kitchen table. He looked across the table and said "How in the hell am I supposed to take a picture of, let alone capture, a sasquatch?"

"Do you have any cookies?" Joey asked. "I think better if I have cookies."

Albert stood, opened the cabinet above his coffee maker and pulled out a new pack of Oreos. He threw them on the table and sat back down.

"Milk?"

Albert sighed, stood up and opened the refrigerator door. He grabbed the milk jug, unscrewed the cap and sniffed. It was still good. He placed the jug on the table and then pulled a plastic cup from the cabinet over his sink. He turned away, then turned back and then retrieved a second cup.

There was no use letting this kid eat cookies alone.

"Okay, you got your cookies. Now, what should I do?"

"So nobody has ever captured a bigfoot before?"

"Sasquatch, Joey. Bigfoot sounds silly and childish."

"I'm seven, Albert. I'm supposed to be silly and childish," Joey informed him.

"Well, grow up kid. This is serious. I told you, if you help me capture this sasquatch, I'll buy you a PlayStation."

"I want an Xbox," Joey negotiated.

"Fine. Now earn it," Albert said, as he twisted two halves of an Oreo, revealing the creamy center. These were Double Stufs. He began licking the thick layer of cream.

"Did you ever play Fortress Attack?" Joey asked.

Albert hadn't even told him about Jamie Booth and his iconic on-line game. The kid just hit on the game on his own, because he played it with his friends. Joey used his mom's computer more than she did.

"Yeah. I've played once or twice. Why?"

"It's October, and it's getting chillier. So use that to your advantage," the kid instructed.

Albert was still lost. Joey could tell by the look on his face.

The young boy began his explanation, "You probably didn't play enough to make it through too many levels. Otherwise, you would know, in level twenty-one you get the infrared scope for your sniper rifle. You can point it at buildings and see the people moving inside because of their body heat."

"Keep going, kiddo, I'm trying to keep up with you," Albert said, slightly annoyed that this kid was so damn smart.

"I assume a bigfoot puts off body heat like a person. Just go out in the cold woods with a heat scope, like in the game. You should be able to see it, if it is around," Joey insisted.

Albert was in awe. This kid was a genius. When this was all over, he might buy him a PlayStation and an Xbox.

Albert sent the kid home full of Oreos and milk. Maybe Joey's mom would see how well he took care of the boy and offer to sleep with him again. They were about due for a night of passion, after the kid went to bed, of course. He made a mental note to work on her a bit.

He fired up his laptop to check on the cost of infrared lenses for his cameras. It didn't take him long to determine that true thermal imaging lenses were way beyond his means. He now had his ninety-five-thousand-dollar windfall, but he was so behind on so many of his bills that he knew it would be half gone before he had a chance to enjoy it. And then there would be taxes.

Besides, he reasoned that it really wasn't necessary for the thermal imaging to be attached to his camera. It was only a means of finding the beast.

He determined he needed a thermal imaging gun or scanner that would have a range of about fifty yards, but that range requirement made those units cost prohibitive as well. But he was never one to quit, so he brainstormed about how to get his hands on a decent imager. His answer was slow to come, but when it did, he felt foolish that he hadn't thought of it sooner.

He grabbed his cellphone and dialed. It rang three times.

A petulant man answered, "Scott here. It's your dime."

"Scott, this is your cousin, Albert. How are you doing?"

"What do you want? And I must warn you, I don't lend money to family, Albert."

Albert felt himself getting red in the face. Scott had always been a jerk as a kid and apparently, he hadn't changed much. But he desperately needed what he thought Scott may have.

Scott Clarion was a government certified energy efficiency contractor. He inspected various commercial buildings and private residences to suggest ways to conserve energy. He was also utilized in many government facilities, military bases and federal buildings.

Scott would suggest window upgrades, insulation improvements and entire heating and cooling systems where needed. One of the tools of the trade that he utilized quite frequently were thermal imagers, to determine where improvements could be made.

Albert had remembered a Thanksgiving, not in the too distant past, where Scott had monopolized thirty minutes of conversation, explaining how awesome thermal imagers were. Albert even remembered the unusual brand name: Fluke.

If he could just borrow one, from this obnoxious cousin, he would be all set.

"Don't need money, Scott. You're such a card. I just need to borrow a piece of your equipment for about a week."

"And what piece of equipment would that be?"

"A Fluke thermal imager. I have a photography job where it could be useful. Can you hook me up?" Albert asked, and then gritted his teeth, because he knew Scott wouldn't make it easy.

Scott cleared his throat, "You mean you want me to lend you a ten-thousand-dollar piece of equipment, for nothing? And after the way you acted on Thanksgiving a few years ago? You basically called me the most boring person that you ever met. Do you recall that?"

"Yeah, Scott. I was having a bad period back then. I apologize."

"Well, I'll tell you what. When you can actually find Flukes for rent, they go for one hundred and fifty to two hundred dollars a day. I'll rent mine to you for the cousin rate of one hundred dollars a day. Take it or leave it."

"Thanks, Scott. I'll take it."

The first part of his plan was coming together. Or more accurately, the first part of Joey's plan was coming together.

Next he would check the weather report. Obviously, a series of cool days was preferred. The weather had turned unseasonably warm and would begin plummeting in two days. The average daytime temperature was forecasted to drop into the low fifties and stay there for almost a week.

He checked weather off his list and pulled out his backpack. Albert was not a great outdoorsman. He owned a backpack for the sole purpose of trying to impress a girl a few years back. The girl was gone, but the pack remained.

He sat on the edge of his bed. What he was mulling over was whether to pack a gun or not. He didn't own one. Albert didn't really like guns. This assignment, however, may border on the dangerous side of life.

He had already determined that his goal was to get good photographs of the beast. There would be no attempt to capture it. He had run the numbers on renting a vehicle, extra helpers, a strong cage, tranquilizer gun and darts.

Once again, he determined that option to be cost prohibitive. Other men may have gambled the windfall he had just received, realizing that if successful the reward would be astronomical.

But the biggest shortcoming wasn't cash. It was courage. He could get some great photos and become half a million dollars richer without breaking a sweat.

That was an oversimplification. If he got close enough for good photos, he would be close enough to be attacked if the beast took umbrage. So should he take a gun or not?

Eventually, he decided not to, because he would have to borrow one. And he had no experience handling a gun. The image of Barney Fife accidently shooting his gun while it was still in its holster was imprinted on his memory.

Aperture 3

October 16th was a cool, cloudy day over Blue Knob State Park. Individual clouds were not readily discernable. The entire expanse of sky was one shade of gray.

He parked his car at trailhead #3, also called Whisper Trail. Albert was returning to the stand of striped maples, which were the subject of the photo that started this entire adventure.

He stood beside his car, adjusting his backpack. Attached to his belt, he wore the Fluke thermal imaging gun in a special holster that was made just for that purpose. He hand carried his camera bag and began the walk along the trail.

There were no other cars parked in the area, so he assumed he was alone. Today the woods looked totally different than on his first outing. On the day of his initial visit, the sun was shining brightly. The trail and forest floor had been sun dappled and a light breeze playing through the leaves had created the appearance of constant movement, as if the forest were alive.

Today, the wind was lighter, but there were no shadows. Everything appeared to be washed in gray. Even the fall colors seemed muted by the cloud filtered light. For a photographer with a keen understanding of color theory and the natural palette of fall, it was disappointing.

He stopped several times along the way, and he pulled the thermal imager and pointed it. He had captured the body heat of scampering squirrels and hopping rabbits. On one occasion, picked out the heat image of a doe standing in the midst of a few oaks.

Forty-five minutes after leaving his car, he stood before the stand of striped maples. In this light, they were totally unremarkable. He was sure that even one of his enhanced filters would not have improved upon the scene.

He pointed the thermal imager and spun in a circle. A few small mammals and a larger bird or two were all that he saw. He knew in his heart that finding the sasquatch here again would be like lightning striking in the same place twice.

He willed himself to move farther down the trail. Albert even questioned the wisdom of staying on the trail. If sasquatches were as reclusive as reported, then expecting one to be walking near man-made trails was sheer folly.

The problem was, however, that he lacked the courage to leave the trail for fear of getting lost. As a child, he remembered being lost in a shopping mall. He was terrified, even though rivers of humanity flowed around him, but they were all strangers.

Out here, if one loses their way, they would only have themselves to rely upon. His self-confidence was not up to the task.

He repeated the litany, "Five hundred thousand dollars," over and over again. He was hoping his love of money would bolster his mettle, but so far it wasn't working.

After another twenty minutes along the trail, he stopped to eat a granola bar. The bars were made by the Amish and sold at a farmer's market just south of Wexford. They were Albert's favorite vice.

It sounded far healthier than it actually was. They contained rolled oats, dates, maple syrup, almonds and chocolate chips, and all were combined to produce the best thing he ever tasted. Whenever Albert made it to the farmer's market, he would buy them out.

He had several more with him in a resealable bag. He had heard that bears would attack hikers and campers that were sloppy with their food. He had no intention of falling victim to any animals on this trip, especially the sasquatch.

He walked along the trail another mile. It was starting to rise in elevation. He scanned the area with his thermal imager.

He spotted another deer, about thirty yards away, and several small mammals, but nothing to warrant excitement or fear.

It was almost 1:00 p.m. and he needed to make the decision that could make or break this trip. Sundown would come at 5:02 p.m. and full dark would occur thirty to forty minutes later.

Should he head back to the car, or spend the night in the wilderness, alone? He had a one-man pup tent with him. Albert had no sleeping bag, but he had a folded blanket and a single size rubber air mattress.

He recalled the forecast had predicted a temperature drop into the upper thirties tonight. He was wearing thermal underwear and his winter coat. In addition, he could build a fire.

He checked his watch once more and said, "Half a million bucks, if I can just tough it out tonight and find the sasquatch tomorrow, I'll be golden."

He walked until 4:20 p.m. and found a clearing next to the trail. It was a bit rocky, but he hoped that his air mattress would keep him comfortable.

He did a quick scan. Nothing showed up in a three-hundred-and-sixty-degree spin. It seemed a bit unusual to not see a thing, but maybe the animals were bedding down in preparation for sunset, he mused.

He first set up his pop-up pup tent and secured it to a few small saplings, just in case the wind should pick up whilst he was gathering wood. He then went on a search for firewood and leaves and needles for kindling.

He was no woodsman, but he carried an old Zippo which had belonged to his father. It had the old man's 3rd Marine battalion insignia on its front and Vietnam 1965-1969 on the back. Starting a fire should prove to be easy.

By 5:00 p.m. he was preparing to light the fire. He had hastily made a rock ring. Rocks were plentiful in this area. The kindling caught and he added the smallest pieces of wood that he had gathered. After the smaller pieces became a small blaze, he added larger chunks of the firewood.

The warmth of the fire was greatly appreciated. The temperature had dropped quickly after the sun disappeared from the Pennsylvania sky.

He sat next to the fire and listened to the wood crackle, pop and sizzle. He also heard at least one owl and the far-off howls from the non-indigenous coyotes that were brought in from western states to cull the deer population.

The next sound that he noticed was the staccato sound of odd clicks. In his mind, he acknowledged that *clicks* wasn't quite the right word. What was he hearing?

He listened intently. It sounded like a thick branch whacking against the trunk of a tree. It was a sound he knew well, from his trips to his grandparents' house.

He had played in the woods behind their home many times. One of the things he liked to do was make the trees sing, that was what he had called it.

Finding a thick stick, he would pound on the skinnier trees. Thick trees absorbed too much of the impact, but the younger trees let loose with a woody, thudding tone. He would go from tree to tree and listen to the different tonal qualities and, if he were lucky, he would find three or four trees that enabled him to play a rhythmic tune.

Yes, he decided that was what it was. Only then did he think about who might be out here pounding on the trees. After what seemed a long time of listening to the melodic thuds, they stopped and were replaced by the strangest howl or shrill growl that he had ever heard.

A chill ran down his spine, and he realized the hairs on the back of his neck were standing up. He was scared, there was no doubt. He wished he would have borrowed someone's gun after all.

The thought almost amused him. The best he could do would be to hold up his Sony wireless flash and blind his assailant. He was sure a bullet would be more effective.

Images of Barney Fife continued to dance in his head. Albert and guns were not a good fit, of course, neither was getting eaten by a sasquatch.

He kept the fire going. Retiring to his tent would make him more vulnerable than he wanted to be. The thin nylon walls would afford him no protection against man nor beast. He wished he had returned to his car.

The night was getting chillier. He began to think that maybe he should have built two fires. Whatever part of him that faced the fire was warm, and conversely, the part facing away from his coveted heat source was freezing.

His thermal underwear and winter coat were being seriously challenged. The light breeze wasn't helping, and that was the one thing his tent could protect him against.

He threw his last pieces of wood on the fire and retired to his nylon cocoon.

As he lie down on his air mattress, he let out a short groan. It was as cold as a slab of granite. He could feel the chill in his legs, through his pants and his thermal underwear.

He covered himself with the blanket, hoping it might be a magic blanket and actually provide warmth. It did not.

He spoke aloud, "I can see the headline in the Pittsburgh Post-Gazette: Local Photographer Dies of Exposure at State Park."

He tossed and turned for almost thirty minutes, and then he heard the loud snap of a nearby twig. It made him jump.

What would be roaming around after dark in these woods? What would be heavy enough to snap twigs?

He made a mental list: a mountain lion, a bear looking to fatten up for hibernation by eating a photographer, and let's not forget, a sasquatch pissed to high heaven that a human was intruding on his territory.

He heard another twig snap and then crunching of other forest detritus underfoot. It was getting closer. He could see through his nylon walls that the light of the fire had died down to almost nothing.

He wished he really could see more than shadow and light through the nylon walls of his little pop-up tomb. At least then he could see what was going to kill him.

There was a plus side to being as scared as he was. He was no longer cold. Or rather, he was cold, but he didn't care.

He heard what sounded like sniffing outside his tent. This was maddening. He wanted to scream like a little girl and have someone come rescue him. He had no illusions of being macho. He was a skinny, mild-mannered photographer who wanted to live to a ripe old age.

Something brushed against his tent.

He curled into the fetal position and willed himself to become smaller, or better yet, invisible.

Time stretched on slowly.

Aperture 4

He awoke, feeling cold and achy. A patch of coldness radiated from left side of his face. He removed his glove and touched his chin. Albert had drooled and the moisture, as it evaporated, felt like it was freezing on his skin.

He didn't need to be Lieutenant Columbo to figure out that he had fallen asleep.

"I'm still alive," he whispered aloud.

He had read about how some people, in terrifying circumstances, turned to sleep to escape. He thought it sounded ridiculous, but he believed that he had just did that exact thing.

He was coiled up in a ball, waiting for death to claim him, but it didn't. Only then did it occur to him to see what time it was. Maybe he had only napped for a short time.

Albert checked his cellphone. There was no signal to make a call, but it still kept time. It was 5:06 a.m. and that meant he had slept almost eight hours.

He felt a great motivation to unzip his tent and rush out to face the world. His courage was at an all-time high, and he had the need to urgently urinate.

He cautiously exited the nylon enclosure. He scanned the area quickly. Nothing. He ran about twenty feet away, unzipped his pants, fought to find the opening in his thermal underwear, and peed so hard he thought he was going to be lifted off the ground.

He sighed with relief when he was done. Packing himself back up, he zipped and went back to his tent. He pulled out his backpack and camera bag, deflated his air mattress and folded his blanket.

He was ready to continue his hike, but first he ate another one of his Amish granola bars. He saw little hoof marks in the non-rocky areas of last night's camp. He guessed it was feral pigs that had come through this area.

Albert had read about the animals before his first trip here. Bedford County had a few small herds of the creatures and some had been spotted in Blue Knob State Park.

Now he personally had proof of their existence. He wondered if they were still around. Using his thermal imager, he checked the surrounding area.

Bingo. A group's heat images appeared just north of his position. At least he thought it was them.

He attached his telephoto lens, put it in his bag and headed in their direction.

It watched him from a distance.

Albert got within twenty yards of the wild pigs as they were rooting around in a small clearing. Opening his camera bag, he withdrew his camera with the telephoto lens and started taking awesome pictures of the elusive swine herd.

It marveled at the thing that the creature pressed against his face and looked through. It watched how he held it and memorized the actions of his fingers.

There was no comprehension of what the process was producing or accomplishing. It just looked intriguing. And the object of the actions were obviously the small, good tasting animals in the clearing.

Its kind had no real language, only grunts and growls attached to deep emotion. For millennia, it had sufficed for the lonely creatures.

They warned each other off by banging branches against trees. Territorial boundaries were sacred. They violated those boundaries only when females were in estrous in the springtime.

Fighting over females did occur, but it was a rare event.

Right now, the beast wanted to watch the interesting creature. He had seen their kind all his life. He had learned which were male and which were female, but some presented as just the opposite. They were confusing creatures to watch at times.

He had killed several over the years. He hadn't decided about this one yet.

After he had tired of photographing the feral pigs, Albert began hiking again. Along the way, beautiful scenery opened up before him and more picture taking ensued.

Along the way, he saw deer and a black bear. The Fluke and the telephoto lens were becoming an unbeatable combination for catching wildlife photos. The cold weather was also supplying some primo leaf changing color.

Albert was so enthralled by his good fortune that he almost forgot that he was looking for the sasquatch.

The sasquatch's curiosity was making it a bit agitated. It wanted to know what the creature was doing with the thing he was holding and fingering.

This was his territory, and he wanted what the creature had. He made up his mind.

This bundled up creature would die and give up the secret of his black box. Soon.

Albert used his Fluke imager and did another three-hundred-and-sixty-degree scan.

"Oh shit!" he whispered aloud. He saw the sasquatch in the imager. The sasquatch had no clue it had been spotted.

Without the imager, Albert could not see the beast. It either was blending well, or it was behind a tree. He squinted, and then he brought the camera up to his face to see if the magnifying lens would help in spotting the legendary animal.

The king of the forest animals saw that the bundled one was pointing his black box his way. Fear shot through it like a lightning strike.

It howled and growled and shrieked in rage and burst through the concealment it had found, heading towards the interloper.

Before Albert could react, the beast was on him. Its great running strides covered thirty yards in less than four seconds.

Albert dropped his camera, without having taken a single picture of the charging beast. He tried to run.

The beast grabbed him by the nape of his neck and threw him aside. Albert hit his shoulder against a tree, and pain shot down his arm.

He tried getting up, but the monster hit him with a closed fist between his shoulder blades. His injured shoulder caused him to scream until he discovered he was out of breath from the crushing blow.

Right there on Whisper Trail, the animal tore Albert asunder, showing no mercy. Its rage was like a growing inferno.

When its anger was spent, it was covered in Albert's blood. It began licking its fur, like a cat that was grooming itself.

And then it began searching for the object of its desire, the black box. It lay clear of the area where Albert was destroyed.

It picked it up, turning it over in its hands. It had observed its use for well over two hours.

It pressed a button and nothing happened. It pressed a second button with its enormous fingers, and the camera whirred to life. The digital camera's viewing screen came to life. The man-like animal stared in amazement.

It turned in a circle, like it had seen Albert do several times. The picture on the back changed, as it moved the box. It noticed that the picture was a smaller version of the real-life view in front of it. Albert never liked that, but instead had always used the viewfinder, like on a regular SLR camera.

When Albert had dropped the camera, the telephoto lens had fallen off. The huge creature would not have understood the magnified image.

It pointed the black box at large rocks by the trail's edge. Mimicking what it had seen Albert do, it pressed a button and the camera made an artificial shutter sound. The rock was recorded on the smart card inside the camera.

It then pointed it at the decimated body of Albert Clarion.

Aperture 5

Linda and Christy loved walking on Whisper Trail in the fall. It was so beautiful as the leaves displayed the beauty associated with their demise.

Reds, oranges, golds, browns and yellows were making the forest appear as a canvas in the hands of an artist of great renown. And Linda insisted that the artist was God himself.

Christy, not as inclined to acknowledge the beauty of God's handiwork, would always smile. Linda said it every year, and they had done their fall trek for fourteen years.

Several miles in, the women found reason to never walk this trail again, as they found the remains of Albert Clarion. Both women became ill.

Having no cell reception in this part of the park, they returned to their car as fast as they could and drove to the ranger's station at the entrance.

The rangers took down every bit of information that the women supplied. Because this appeared to be an animal attack, two rangers, instead of one, went to investigate.

Within hours, an ambulance and a medical examiner's vehicle were on scene. The responders were told there was no reason for a gurney. Body bags would be sufficient.

The EMTs admitted to one another that this was the most gruesome scene they had ever witnessed. Both had responded to many horrific events by which to gauge what they were currently viewing.

Photos were recorded, measurements taken and evidence collected. The main pieces of evidence were the bloodstained backpack, the badly broken Fluke thermal imager, the camera bag filled with smart cards and lens cleaning paraphernalia, the shattered telephoto lens and the camera itself.

Ranger Dave Champion was the man assigned to do the investigation. A death in the park was a serious matter, and Champion was the senior ranger on site.

He enlisted the help of Ranger Jill Parker, to assist him in analyzing the evidence. Their first job was to determine what kind of animal had attacked the man.

Several hairs were bagged and sent to Penn State University for analysis. None of the rangers were sure what they were from, and none cared to venture a guess. The reason was simple. They knew what the hairs were not.

They were not mountain lion or bear. They were not feral pig bristles, but something completely different. The elephant in the investigation room was a mythical beast that most people agreed did exist. Hopefully, the scientific analysis would yield some truth.

Dave had asked Jill to scan through the pictures on the camera's smart card. She set aside some time and began looking them over.

She commented to Dave that this guy was a really good photographer. He captured proof of the existence of the feral hogs. He took some beautiful photos of the ugly things.

As they talked back and forth, Dave said, "Once we can identify what animal with which we are dealing, we can start wrapping up this incident. Frankly, I'm going to vote for a bear, how about you?"

"It didn't seem like bear hair, but maybe there is a scientific explanation for that. And I'm hoping sasquatch isn't it. There I said it."

Dave laughed, "It's what we all were thinking, Jill. You are not alone. There will be a reasonable explanation, I'm sure. At least it wasn't a homicide. Now that would be a huge mess, and we'd have to call the Pennsylvania State Pain in the Asses. They'd probably close down the park."

He noticed as he was talking, Jill seemed mesmerized by what she had on her computer screen. He could see the light reflected off her face and saw her finger clicking at her mouse. The light appeared to signify that she was switching back and forth between to images, over and over.

"Jill, what's wrong?"

"I'm afraid you are going to have to call the Pennsylvania State Police after all," she answered.

He got up from his desk and walked over to stand behind her. She was bouncing back and forth between, what appeared to be, two crime scene photos.

"My God! Whoever took those photos had not a single clue about framing and composition. Why are you looking at crime scene photos? Are you done with the camera's smart card?"

"Dave," she began, "this *is* the smart card."

"You mean, someone stood over the body and took those two pictures?" he asked, incredulously.

"Yep. Appears so."

Dave went to the phone on his desk, and looking down, he began dialing a number.

Jill could only hear Dave's end of the conversation.

"Yes, hello. Is this Linda Furnier?"

"This is Ranger Champion, from Blue Knob State Park. We spoke earlier. Just a quick question that I failed to ask earlier. Did either you or your friend, Christy, pick up Mr. Clarion's camera?"

There was a short pause.

"I see. I'm sorry to have bothered you, and I'm sorry you had to have such an unpleasant experience here in our park. Thank you for your time."

Dave hung up and sat, staring at the large desktop calendar that he used as a desk pad.

Jill couldn't wait any longer, "Well, what did she say?"

"They didn't even know there was a camera. It wasn't them. Obviously, Clarion's killer took the pictures," Dave said in summation.

Jill wasn't sure how she felt about what that meant. A monster of nature or a human monster, both would keep people away from the park.

"What we have, plain and simple, is a homicide. There is a maniac on the loose. How one human being can do that to another is beyond me. We need to call in the State Police."

"Should I gather the evidence and do the paperwork for the transfer of custody?" she asked.

"Yes."

The Pennsylvania State Police took over the case. It was one of their most confusing cases on record.

The hairs that were sent to Penn State University were identified as Animalia-Chordata-Mammalia-Primate-Simiformes and then the classification stopped. The markers beyond infraorder became muddy and indistinct, as in, never classified before.

The excitement concerning the hairs was quite extraordinary. Researchers were split between claiming whatever the creature may be, as in the family Hominidae, or calling that too far a leap without more conclusive proof.

The Pennsylvania State Police examined all the evidence. All bloodstains and residue belonged exclusively to Albert Clarion. A few more hairs were recovered, but they proved no different than those already examined.

The camera became the main focus of the investigation. They took exhaustive measurements and calculations concerning the angle of the photos of the dead man. The resulting conclusion was that the camera was held seven and one half to eight feet high when the photos were taken.

No one was exactly sure what that meant, if anything.

Next, the camera was dusted for prints and any other evidence that might be gleaned.

Over three dozen fingerprints were pulled from the photographic device. All of them belonged to Albert

Clarion, except two. But there was a problem with those--the size.

If the results were to be believed, the prints were three to four times the size of human fingerprints, as if a giant had taken a turn taking photos once Clarion was finished.

The case was never solved.

Sightings of Big Blue continued, and the occasional hiker, camper and/or fisherman went missing from time to time.

What Albert Clarion had captured in his original photo was meant to be left alone. What he sought, destroyed him.

Dear reader, please let this be a cautionary tale.

The TV

Channel 1

Daryl looked at Tim and said, "Seriously, you're packing a solar powered TV on our camping trip?"

"Why not? There's only so much sitting around and watching trees grow that a man can take. I can watch TV and enjoy the fresh air at the same time. Besides, we get there Saturday, and I'll do whatever you want. But Sunday, I'll want to watch football. And on Monday night and Thursday night, I'll be doing it too." Tim responded.

"You really know how to rough it, buddy. You bringing a solar powered microwave too? That way we can make popcorn, nachos and wings for the football games," Daryl teased.

"Microwaves consume too much power for solar to be effective. So, I'm packing enough Twinkies, Doritos and pretzel sticks to see me through. Just make sure you have enough beer when you pick me up Saturday morning," Tim instructed.

On Saturday morning, Daryl picked Tim up, just as planned. Their week in the woods had begun. For the two brothers, this was their annual trip.

It used to include their father, but he had died from pancreatic cancer four years earlier. The brothers continued the camping tradition.

Daryl was the outdoorsman of the two. Tim continued the tradition just to be close to his brother, whom he rarely saw, except at their mom's house on Easter, Thanksgiving and Christmas.

Tim wasn't a complete couch potato. He exercised regularly at a gym and played pickleball with friends. But he did enjoy watching sports, and this week's camping trip was not going to stop him from doing that.

They were not camping too remotely. The plan was always the same. They entered Rothrock State Forest and travelled into the woods about seven miles on Logging Road 11.

They stopped at the same spot every year. The logging road continued, but became much more treacherous beyond their stopping point. In fact, even getting back to their favorite spot became more of a challenge each trip. The logging roads ceased to be maintained decades ago.

One year, their dad, who always packed his chainsaw for firewood, actually got to use it for something else. A medium-sized tree had fallen across the road, and their father jumped into action and cut a section, a little wider than the road, into small enough pieces to be easily moved. Once the road was made passable, they continued their adventure.

They dubbed the fallen tree, Dad's Pass. And they noted it every trip. The trunk still remained, with its flat sliced ends bracketing the old road as they drove between them. Their father's handiwork was immortalized for years to come.

On this trip, Tim asked, "How many other people do you think have passed between those sawed off ends of dad's tree?"

"Going by the condition of this road, not that many," Daryl answered. "But it's enough that we drive through every year. It reminds me of that day. The old man was so happy to finally get to use his chainsaw for something other than just firewood."

The two men reached their destination. After twenty minutes of policing their campsite area of sticks, branches and a few rocks, they set up their tent.

"How do rocks move?" Tim asked.

Daryl looked at his brother like he was a lunatic.

Tim rolled his eyes, which he was in the habit of doing whenever Daryl failed to understand him.

Tim explained, "We set up the tent in the same spot every year, and every year we end up removing more rocks before we set it up. Where are they coming from?"

Daryl's face showed a bit of animation, "Damn! You're right. We just tossed about seven or eight rocks to get them out of the way. By rights, after all these years, this area should be rock free."

"See. It wasn't a stupid question. It's like that place out west where the rocks move. It is called The Racetrack, and it's in Death Valley. It's really cool," Tim declared.

"So how do those rocks move?" Daryl asked.

"It is an area that is perfectly flat and baked hard and cracked on the surface. In the winter, it rains and then the water freezes on the surface. When the temperature rises above freezing, the ice on the surface of The Racetrack cracks and pushes the rocks forward. Over time, the process creates a clear trail behind the rock," Tim explained excitedly.

"So that kind of crap really floats your boat, little brother?" Daryl asked, a bit mockingly.

"Yes. Science, reading books and educating myself makes me happy. So how are you and your comic books coming along?" Tim said, zinging his brother.

Daryl just gave him the finger and walked away to get the cooler out of his Jeep Cherokee.

Tim joined him in unpacking the vehicle.

After they finished setting up their camp, Daryl convinced Tim to take a short hike. They had a favorite spot where a huge outcropping of rock opened up into a cave. They never missed the opportunity to check out the cave.

In past years, they had found remnants of what appeared to be a homeless person taking up shelter in the cave. Of course, Tim added dramatic flair to their findings by supposing it was a fugitive from the law that had held up there.

Daryl always marveled at his younger brother's imagination. He himself was an outdoors adrenaline junkie. He wasn't into traditional team sports, but rather, he enjoyed climbing, rappelling, whitewater rafting and the occasional bungee jump.

Daryl dealt in facts and had very little flair in embellishing anything beyond factual description. Tim often referred to him as Joe Friday from the Dragnet television series. *Just the facts, ma'am* was his favorite catchphrase.

It wasn't that Daryl had no imagination. It was just that he needed more time and motivation to get his creative juices flowing. Tim was just much quicker in that regard.

The cave was empty this time. There was some bear scat nearby, and both brothers wondered if a bear might have taken up temporary residence there.

"It doesn't appear that fresh. It probably moved on. It's only the first week in October. No self-respecting bear would be caught hibernating this early. The bears are still chubbing up," Tim stated.

Chubbing up was what their dad used to call it, when bears were increasing their caloric in-take for hibernation. They didn't know why he called it that, but he thought it was cute, and he used the term when they came on their annual fall camping trip.

It was just another of many memories their camping trip invoked every year. Fond memories. Sometimes the trip became melancholic as the memories came flooding back. But neither of the brothers was willing to stop it from happening. Their dad had been a special part of their lives.

Back at camp, they gathered wood for a fire. It was necessary to fire up their dad's old chainsaw to cut the wood into more usable sizes. They never cut down anything live. The brothers used only what was already dead and littering the forest floor. There was always enough.

Once the fire was going, they popped the tops off of two beers. They sat down to get warm and reminisce about the old days when all three of them were together. The melancholy was kicking in early.

It was Daryl who broke the spell, "You know, dad would be appalled that you brought that damn TV."

"I brought it because, without dad, you're not capable of holding up your end of an intellectual conversation," Tim said, smiling from ear to ear.

Daryl's response was a curt, "Bite me."

The sun set at about 5:07 p.m. and shortly thereafter, the temperature rapidly dipped.

The night passed peacefully.

Channel 2

It was Sunday morning, and Tim fired up his TV. He found Charles Stanley preaching the Word. He forced Daryl to watch the old preacher.

That was another difference between the brothers. Tim was a committed Christian, and Daryl leaned more to the agnostic side.

Daryl did not reject the faith his parents had taught him, he just chose to reserve his obeisance for Easter, Christmas and Thanksgiving, when his mom insisted upon it.

Tim rarely missed Sunday church services with his fiancée, Gail. Daryl was still playing the field, but Tim and his mom prayed he would find a good woman of faith. They knew that a truly good woman could get a man like Daryl to come to church without kicking and screaming the whole way.

After Charles Stanley delivered his low-key words of truth, Tim switched to the endless hours of pregame analysis. He loved Howie, Terry, Jimmy, Michael and Curt. They made the analysis fun to watch.

The games eventually started, and Tim was lost in football until almost midnight. Daryl watched for a while, but lost interest.

He had gathered wood for the evening fire. He also fetched water from a nearby creek. The water was clear, cool and was used for their supper.

Daryl cooked so that Tim could watch uninterrupted football. He was concerned that Tim wouldn't be hungry. He was pounding down the snack food all afternoon, but he took a break to eat some of the beef stroganoff that his brother had prepared.

Daryl occupied himself with an issue of Field and Stream for the balance of the evening. He hit the sack about 8:30 p.m. while Tim finished his football viewing.

Tim finally turned off his TV, smothered the fire and crawled into his sleeping bag. It was perfect sleeping weather as far as Tim was concerned.

Monday was a bit overcast, but the solar powered TV was still recharging. Tim wanted to watch Monday Night Football. He hoped there would be enough of a charge for the entire game.

The hiked for a few hours. They found some more bear scat, but this was fresher than the previous samples they had seen. Unfortunately, neither of them had remembered to bring bear spray.

During their many years of camping, they had experienced only one bear encounter. The poor creature was more afraid of them than they were of it.

Upon returning to their camp, they found their tent had been ripped down and Tim's snacks were strewn all around. Daryl started to scold his little brother for his carelessness, but stopped cold when he saw the bear staring at them.

It was a big one. Daryl guessed it to be at least four hundred pounds and more. He grabbed his brother's arm and whispered, "Tim, bear at one o'clock."

Tim looked to the location his brother described. Fear shot down his back as his body prepared for fight or flight. And flight was going to be the winner.

Daryl whispered, "The Cherokee is unlocked, bro. Let's make a run for it. On three."

The bear stood up on its back legs and roared. It stood at least six and a half feet tall.

Neither brother waited for the count. They both bolted towards the unlocked vehicle. They made it safely inside of the SUV.

Tim looked at his brother, "Please tell me you have your keys."

"Yep. We can get going and come back some other time for our stuff. We're not safe if we stay," Daryl declared.

"Wait! My TV!" Tim protested.

"Little bro, you are welcome to go get it, but my ass stays right here. It's only a cheap TV. It's not even a brand name that I have ever heard of. It's Sonix or some shit. Just forget it," Daryl pleaded.

"You're right. Let's split. Next year we'll bring bear spray," Tim promised.

"After this, I'm not so sure about there being a next year," the older brother remarked.

Daryl started the car, turned onto the logging road and headed out. This annual excursion was over.

Four days later, they returned with bear spray and a rifle. Their intention was to retrieve their property. It was all where they had left it, except Tim's TV. It was missing.

After the brothers had left, the bear rooted around, cleaning up the pieces of Twinkies, Doritos and pretzels it had missed in its first foray.

The bear sat back on its haunches and sniffed the air. A bear this size would normally find itself with no natural enemies, except man. But Rothrock State Forest was different.

The sasquatch was the undisputed king of these forests. The animals knew it, but men had yet to get the memo.

It avoided man at every turn. Its natural instinct told it to back away. But this was a bear, and it was coming to satisfy its curiosity.

As the giant's scent became stronger, the bear growled and scrambled in the opposite direction. It wanted nothing to do with the approaching creature.

The sasquatch arrived at the encampment. It marveled at the things lying in the dirt. It found two Twinkies still in their wrappers. It put one into its mouth to test it.

As it bit down, the wrapper exploded, releasing the spongy cake and cream filling.

"Mmmmm," was all that it could say. It didn't like the feel of the skin, so with its giant hands, it peeled off the plastic of the second one and ate just the cake.

"Mmmmm," was repeated. Had any human observed, they would have been delighted by how human the creature sounded.

It sat down by what had been the brother's fire pit. There were several things to look at and play with. A fry pan, a pot, utensils, a magazine, a mountain pie maker and two telescoping hot dog forks were lying about.

After examining those things, the sasquatch got up and explored the contents inside the tent. The brothers had left several interesting things behind.

In contrast to the yumminess of the Twinkies, the beast made a horrible gagging sound after biting into Tim's deodorant stick.

Moments later, it depressed the top of a can, accidentally, and ended up covered in shaving cream. It tasted that also, with negative results.

Time was passing by, and it was still at the campsite after dark. It decided to take a short nap.

At 7:30 p.m. the solar TV popped on. Tim had set the timer, not wanting to chance missing any of the pregame Monday night coverage.

The big beast jumped up, stepped back and snarled at the device. It played on as the sasquatch overcame its fear and allowed its curiosity to take over.

The giant was enthralled, watching the little humans chatter on and on. While Tim was at home watching the game, the sasquatch was watching it also.

There was no real comprehension of why the little people wore matching outfits and banged into each other constantly, but it was entertaining. The beast watched the boxy looking TV until it ran out of power.

The legendary monster decided it was time to move, but first it grabbed the TV. It wanted to see more.

Channel 3

The next three years found Tim and Daryl continuing to enjoy their annual trip. For safety sake, they each brought a rifle and bear spray.

The mystery of the missing TV continued to bother Tim. He figured some hiker or hunter came along and benefitted from his loss. He learned to not bring anything expensive along again, except his rifle.

They were setting up camp in this third year after *the bear attack*. That is how Daryl referred to it, but Tim reminded him that the bear never really attacked them.

They had learned to be more vigilant when camping. The bear hadn't been seen since.

Without his TV, Tim made himself more available to do the things his brother enjoyed. This afternoon, they were going to practice rappelling off of some short cliffs. It was to be a practice session, to get used to the equipment and safety procedures. It would be a little dangerous, but not too bad. That was Daryl's description, *dangerous, but not too bad*.

The afternoon went as planned, and they returned to camp with no broken bones. Tim did get a nasty rope burn on his left hand and spent some time with the first aid kit.

Daryl, knowing his brother was hurting, volunteered to make a fire and start dinner. Tonight's cuisine would be pad Thai with chicken. Both brothers couldn't get over how good their camping meals were becoming. They believed that the dehydrated meals were getting as good as meals you could find in the freezer section of your local supermarket.

Instead of Twinkies, Tim packed M&Ms in airtight containers. He couldn't get by without his sugar fix. Daryl was never a sweets person. He preferred the raisins and dates he had brought along in his airtight containers.

The smell of dinner filled the air. It made the brothers hungry. They knew it may draw other creatures as well. So, a can of bear spray and a rifle were nearby.

The bigfoot was nearby, and the smell he was picking up was making him salivate. He followed his nose to the camp of the brothers.

This was actually the sixth or seventh time he had seen them over the years. He remembered an older one that used to be with them. He always observed, but never too closely.

They were so much like him. They walked upright and had hands with opposable thumbs. And now, after all these years, he could understand what they were saying.

He watched TV almost every night.

The brothers finished up their meal and continued to sit and warm by the fire.

"So, you ever going to marry Gail?"

"Why? We already live together," Tim responded.

"Aren't you supposed to be a good Christian? Living together goes against your values, doesn't it?" Daryl prodded Tim for a reaction.

"Yes and no. If I was just using her, or felt it was a temporary arrangement, that would be wrong. But I already treat her as my wife and consider her as such. And she is wearing the ring I bought her. So, we are married in the eyes of God."

"Cute answer little brother, but tell me the truth. Why not finish what you started?" Daryl persisted.

"Truth? I'm not sure she is the one," Tim admitted.

Daryl just stared with his mouth agape.

The beast watched them from a distance and could understand some of the things they said. Three years of daily TV watching had made the beast bilingual. Or since sasquatches had no formal language of their own, single lingual.

The sasquatch had caught on fairly quickly that daylight made the TV work and lack of light caused it to black out. He could reason with the best of them, if *them* were described as other sasquatches. Besides men, he was the smartest thing in the forest.

More accurately, he was one of three sasquatches within the boundaries of Rothrock. There were two females with whom he would mate during their estrous periods in the springtime. The females did not like each other.

In truth, they could only stand his presence during the mating season. Then he was the king of the forest. After mating, they would drive him off with angry and sometimes violent behavior.

The two men he was observing were talking about something similar. The younger, taller one with the longer hair just admitted the female he was living with wasn't his forever mate.

It was one thing he learned on TV. Men and women, which is what they were called, attempted to mate for a lifetime. Some were good at it and some were not. Personally, he thought it was silly. One mate for your entire life. That would be miserable.

He based his opinion upon the behavior of the female sasquatches.

"What do you mean she's not the one? You just wasted four years of the poor girl's life! You have to stand up and do the right thing!" Daryl said, with more volume than he intended.

"So, by the right thing, you think I should marry the wrong woman," Tim responded angrily.

"Okay, calm down. Just tell me what she did to change your mind?" Daryl asked.

"She wants to get married by her brother," Tim said disgustedly.

"I didn't know her brother was a minister," Daryl said.

"He's not. He wants to do one of those internet ordination things and then marry us. I don't like that and truth be known, I don't like him. He's a lazy, self-centered asshole."

"Don't use him. Fire his ass," Daryl suggested.

"Can't. She thinks her brother walks on water. And that is what pisses me off the most. She thinks that narcissistic, butthole is a great guy. So, where does that leave me?"

"I'm lost," Daryl admitted.

"Awe, c'mon man. If she likes assholes, then I must be an asshole, right?"

"No, Tim. He's family. That's a whole different category of asshole. Family assholes get a free pass," Daryl explained.

A twig behind them snapped loudly.

Tim grabbed the bear spray, and Daryl grabbed the rifle.

He kept edging forward to hear what they were saying. He heard *assholes* and was trying to gain an understanding of what that meant.

He took one step too many, and a thick twig snapped under his great weight. He looked down and then looked up to see what the men were doing.

He could see the younger one had grabbed a can of some sort, or maybe it was called a canister. The language was so difficult sometimes. The older one grabbed a gun, sometimes called a rifle. This wasn't good.

He needed to diffuse the situation. He stepped forward and said, "Hey!"

Channel 4

The giant came from between two trees and made a noise. Daryl was paralyzed by what he was seeing and never raised the rifle, but Tim sprang into action.

He unloaded the bear spray on the beast.

The giant howled and screamed, "Son of a black bear's butt!" And then gagged and rubbed its eyes.

"Water! Need water!" the beast screamed.

Daryl stepped forward and put a canteen in its left hand.

Tim was incredulous, "What the hell are you doing, Daryl?"

"He screamed for water. So I gave him some."

Tim held his hand palm up and gestured toward the sasquatch, "Monster, bro. That's a fricking monster you're helping."

The sasquatch was looking up, head back and using the canteen water to rinse the pepper spray from its eyes.

"No monster," the large, hairy thing said.

Tim held the bear spray out in front of him, while staring in astonishment. The thing was talking.

"You talk," Tim said, with a slight smile playing across his face.

"Oh, now we're smiling? Just a minute ago you were telling me, fricking monster, like I had just betrayed the human race," Daryl said pointedly.

"Can you men be quiet until I can see again?" the monster requested.

"Why? So you can kill us?" Tim accused.

"No kill. I watch you for hours. Never kill you. For years, even when you were three. Older man was with you. No kill," the bigfoot informed them.

Tim lowered the bear spray, "You saw us with our dad?"

"Yes, dad. If you say so. More water, please," the sasquatch requested.

Daryl had a two-liter bottle of water that he handed to the beast.

It took the water, and said, "Sorry, very much."

"You mean, thank you, very much," Tim corrected.

"Yes. Thank you, very much. Your talk is so hard to know," it said.

"Well, that begs the question, how did you learn it?" Daryl asked.

The beast continued to flush its eyes with the water from the two-liter bottle, and answered, "The TV box."

Tim thought about it for a few seconds, and then said, "You're the one who stole my TV!"

"I found. You left. I take and learn your talk. Good to learn, right?"

Daryl laughed at both the big creature and his little brother.

Tim paused and realized that he wasn't the least bit afraid of this myth come to life. It could end his life and his brother's very easily, but it didn't seem the least bit hostile towards them, and it had observed them for years. If it meant them harm, it had ample opportunity to act.

The giant had finally finished rinsing his eyes. It continued to sniff and clear its throat. The pepper was still causing some discomfort.

Tim saw how uncomfortable it was and apologized for using the pepper spray on him, "Sorry, fella. I thought you meant us harm."

"No harm. No kill. No hurt. Want to be friends. You know, friends?" it asked.

"Yes. We know friends," Daryl answered.

"What is your name?" Tim asked.

"I don't know?"

Daryl and Tim exchanged glances.

"Why don't you know your name?" Daryl asked.

"I no have name. People like me, no have names," the sasquatch said.

"People? You think you are a person?" Tim asked.

"Yes. I am people too. I live, just like you. I am people too."

Tim smiled. He wasn't sure where this conversation should go. This was all so surreal. To see a bigfoot and to find it can talk was overwhelming.

The beast smiled at them. Its big teeth were very square in front and its canines were not very long. They were yellowed a bit, but were relatively clean.

"You are smiling," Daryl said.

"Yes, smile face," the oversized animal agreed.

"What does that mean to you?" Tim asked.

"Nice face. Friend face. Good face. No kill. No hurt."

"Okay, friend. Maybe we should give you a name. Would you like that?" Daryl asked.

"Yes! Yes! Yes! Name. Me pick," it said.

Tim found himself smiling again. This huge thing was so childlike and wanted to be their friend. He couldn't help but like it.

"So, what name would you like?" Tim asked.

"Willy Wonka. Or maybe, Raymond. Everybody loves him. Doogie Howser or Malcom in the Middle could be nice as well. But my favorite is Rudolph, the deer with glow nose. I want Rudolph. Okay?" he asked, like a child looking for approval.

"Sure," Tim said. "Rudolph is a great name. You are now to be known as Rudolph."

Daryl rolled his eyes. He was hoping Willy Wonka would win out.

"Rudolph is hungry. Go hunt now."

With that declaration, the big beast turned, walked away and melted into the woods.

Daryl looked at Tim, "Can you believe this shit? If you would have told me that one day I'd see a bigfoot and remove all doubt of its existence, I would have said you were crazy. But what just happened is off the charts, bro."

"I want my TV back," Tim stated.

"Dude, are you kidding? Rudolph needs to keep watching it, so he can stop talking like a caveman."

"Daryl, he is a caveman. Rudolph is just about the very definition of a caveman. He's not modern man. He is not even Neanderthal. He is a smart animal that has learned to talk. He is an anomaly," Tim stated matter-of-factly.

"Why aren't you more excited about this?" Daryl asked, concerned by his brother's unusual reaction.

"Dad saw him the year before he died. He told me, but made me promise not to tell you. It scared him, and he thought he was hallucinating," Tim remembered.

"Why didn't you guys tell me?"

Tim stared down at his own feet, "Because I told dad it could be a sign of mental problems. Remember, about that time he was having episodes of mild dementia. So when he told me he saw a bigfoot, I told him that it was his mind playing tricks on him. I convinced the poor man he was losing his mind. He didn't want you to know."

"So, he was right. He saw Rudolph, and you thought he was seeing things. It is not your fault, Tim," Daryl said to console his brother.

"He died two months later, and twice during those two months he wanted to talk about it. He told me that what he saw felt different than the mental fugues he was experiencing. I got angry with him both times and shut him down. The poor guy just wanted to talk about it, and I made him feel like dirt," Tim said in a pained voice.

Daryl wasn't sure how to help him, but asked, "Why is that making you mad at Rudolph?"

A tear rolled down Tim's cheek, "He is a living reminder of how I mistreated our father, right before he died. And the old man was right, and I was terribly wrong.

"I know it's not Rudolph's fault, but it hurts and makes me angry all the same."

"Then let me do the talking around our new, amazing friend. He just wants to make friends. Even if he is an anomaly, this is the most fantastic thing to ever happen to us."

"How do you know he won't kill us?" Tim asked.

"Tim, he could have already done that," Daryl responded truthfully. The beast could have killed them at any time, with very little effort.

"You can't tell anyone. No one at all. If you do, they'll come here and capture him and ruin his life. Maybe even kill him in the process," Tim informed his brother. He was right. Men would turn the miracle to mush by their meddling.

"Fine. I just want to talk to him and learn what I can."

"Agreed," Tim said. "I'll set aside my emotions and learn from this. I promise."

Channel 5

They were sitting around the fire when Rudolph returned. He came crashing through the underbrush. It caused the brothers to both jump up, Daryl holding his rifle and Tim holding his bear spray.

Rudolph saw Tim and screamed. He covered his face with his arms, "No spray! No spray! It's me, Rudolph! Me Rudolph!"

Tim lowered the spray can and began to laugh, "Easy, big boy. I'll put it down."

Daryl lowered his rifle, "Thought you were a bear, buddy."

"No bear. If me here, bear no here. Afraid of me," he said, almost proudly.

"Rudolph, sit by the fire. I have many questions to ask you," Tim told him.

"Me too. Me have lots and lots. So much me don't understand. You help me, sorry."

"You help me, please. Not sorry. Got it?" Tim corrected.

"Me get. What question you ask?" Rudolph inquired.

"How many of your kind are there?" Daryl chimed in.

Rudolph's brows were knitted. He was obviously thinking and then said, "Me no understand numbers well. Me know two is this many and one, this many," he said, first holding up two fingers and then one.

Tim hadn't thought about concepts such as numbers that were foreign to the beast.

"For each of the other sasquatch that you know about, because that is what you are, a sasquatch, show me a finger for each one," Tim instructed.

Daryl leaned closer. He was beyond curious.

"Sasquatch. Me sasquatch. Funny word," the beast mused.

"Come on, Rudolph. How many? One finger for each one," Tim prodded.

Rudolph held up three fingers.

"Only three?" Daryl questioned.

Rudolph saw his disappointment, and Tim's too.

"Me make babies with two. And one man sasquatch, I scare away many, many hot and cold times ago."

Tim looked at Daryl, "This is going to be exhausting for all of us. What the hell is a hot and cold time?"

Daryl was on it, "He means summers and winters. Basically, years ago. And man sasquatch is a male of his kind. But why only three, if he has children?"

"What about your children? Your babies?" Tim asked.

"Never see. You said that me see. My birther, who make me. Birther died. Did not count her," the giant clarified.

Tim said to Daryl, "The woods could be filled with his offspring."

"No. No babies, children, in my forest. Me would know," Rudolph assured them.

"Rudolph, stop using *me* incorrectly. You want to use the word I. I would know, not me would know," Tim corrected again.

"Brother, if you keep correcting his grammar, this is going to be exhausting," Daryl whined.

They talked into the wee hours of the morning.

Eventually, the brothers went to bed, and Rudolph walked back to a cave in which he had lived for several decades.

All the questions on this evening had come from the brothers. Tomorrow would be Rudolph's turn to ask questions.

What Daryl and Tim learned was the following.

Sasquatch are lone animals, except during mating season, which is every other spring. They presumed that since the mating seasons were two years apart, or two cold seasons would pass according to Rudolph, pregnancy was longer in these animals.

The nearest sasquatch were two females, and both mated with Rudolph. It was presumed that there were many years of live births, but once the offspring were launched from the nest, they would run off to claim their own territory in the woods.

The sasquatch avoid humans instinctively. Rudolph did not have a reason, other than a natural fear of exposure.

The giant did not believe he had ever been seen by humans, until now. Tim informed him that his father saw him on one of their camping trips.

Rudolph had asked why they didn't come looking for him. They did their best to explain that they didn't believe he existed. It was a hard concept for him to grasp, not being believed to exist.

Rudolph, believing he had never been seen by a human, had obviously never hurt a human. He did, however, fight both bears and cougars and lived to tell the story. He said cougars were the worst because they used their claws very quickly and could cause great damage. Rudolph showed them some scars.

He and the females were the undisputed royalty of the forest, but they had fought hard to be so.

They had no formal language of their own, nor did they possess socialization skills. But watching humans had touched off a yearning within the beast to make friends with something, anything. They learned that he had a pet deer for a while, until a cougar ate it. The cougar paid dearly, according to their big friend.

That gave the brothers an idea to get him a dog. They were not sure what kind, but it would have to be a good outdoor dog. Daryl and Tim would work on that, once they got back to civilization.

Finding the TV allowed Rudolph to see what socialization looked like, good and bad. They couldn't wait to hear what questions he had for them.

Tim no longer wished to get his television back. In fact, he had suggested that they should get him a new one. The thinking was that a new TV would help further his education.

Their last hour together was difficult. Rudolph had suggested that he couldn't wait to meet other humans. Internal alarms went off for the brothers.

They spent the rest of the evening trying to explain to Rudolph why that would be a bad idea. The big beast just didn't know how special he was and how dark and twisted men could be.

The brothers were afraid that either science would want to dissect him, the military would try to weaponize him or some greedy bastard would try to use him to get rich. They didn't want other people to take advantage of his humanity, and that sparked a long discussion between the two siblings.

Rudolph was becoming human to them. A human child. He was a giant human toddler with so much to learn.

Channel 6

The next day, Rudolph showed up about mid-morning. He had some fresh blood on his matted fur. He told the brothers he had just eaten half a fresh deer. The other half was waiting back in his cave for later.

Deer are incredibly fast, which prompted Daryl to ask, "How can you run as fast as a deer to catch it?"

Rudolph shook his head no, "Don't run. I am fast, but deer faster. Or me am fast?"

Tim grinned, "No. You were correct. I am fast is good."

Rudolph smiled, looking very pleased with himself.

Daryl couldn't stand the constant grammar corrections. He understood Rudolph perfectly, and he wanted an answer.

"So how do you catch the deer?" Daryl asked, getting the big beast back on track.

"Rocks." That was all he said, and then he bent over, picked up a two- or three-pound stone and pointed at a squirrel. It was sitting on a branch about sixty feet away, on the other side of the logging road.

Both brothers looked, "The squirrel?" Tim asked.

"Yep," he said and let the rock fly.

The squirrel never had a chance. The rock made impact with the squirrel and the branch at the same time. They saw the little creature plummet to the ground.

The sasquatch ran to where the squirrel had fallen and picked it up and walked back to them.

"This is snack. Like you eat tato chips," he said, and then bit off the top half of the squirrel and swallowed it. Little trails of blood ran down the sides of his mouth into what could only be described as his beard.

Tim had to turn away. He found it nauseating.

Daryl, on the other hand, found it fascinating. He would later describe it as, like watching a train wreck. He just couldn't look away.

Tim grabbed a wad of paper towels out of the car and some water from his canteen and washed off Rudolph's face. Amazingly, the huge, man-like animal just sat there and let him do it.

"When you answer I questions?" Rudolph asked.

"No. When will you answer *my* questions," Tim corrected.

"Me answered," Rudolph stopped and restarted. "I answered your questions day before today."

Daryl started laughing so hard he snorted.

Tim shook his head no, "I was correcting you, not asking about more questions. You're supposed to say, when will you answer *my* questions, not *I* questions."

"I thought you said no use me?" Rudolph questioned.

"Me is not the same as my," Tim said.

Daryl touched Tim's shoulder, "This isn't the time for a grammar lesson. Please stop. We understand him and right now, that is amazing enough."

Tim could feel his neck getting red. He knew Daryl was right and didn't know why he was being so anal about the grammar of this miracle in front of them.

"Go ahead and ask your questions, Rudolph," Tim instructed.

The monster smiled. He was still digging its name.

"Why is the news so scary? Every news show scary. Men and woman hurt each other. Kill each other. One herd hate another herd. Why?"

Tim looked at Daryl, "How do we explain that? It isn't supposed to be that way."

"Rudolph," Daryl began, "you protect the forest that belongs to you, right?"

"Yes. Me protect forest," he looked at Tim. "I mean, I protect forest."

Tim nodded and smiled and Rudolph beamed.

"Men have lots of different forests they protect. Men like their own herd, but not other herds. Do you understand?" Daryl asked.

The big beast cocked his head, in what could only be described as a quizzical manner.

"Rudolph, men find all kinds of reasons not to like each other. And men belong to more than one herd. That means there are more herds to dislike, as well. Now do you understand?" Daryl hoped he was getting it.

"You say, men don't like other men for many, uh, reasons?" Rudolph paraphrased.

Tim listened as the beast displayed an astonishing level of cognitive thinking.

"Yes! You get it. That dislike for each other makes men do dumb things and that's news," Daryl said in summation.

Rudolph seemed to understand.

"More questions, buddy?" Tim asked.

"Why does everybody love Raymond? He is not always nice. His mate yells and call him idiot. Not nice name, okay?" he asked.

"That is humor. I'm not sure you can understand what that is. Raymond isn't always lovable, and that is why it is sometimes funny," Tim answered.

Whether he understood or not, they would not know. He countered with his next question, "Why is Seinfeld TV show about nothing? It always seems to be something, but they say it about nothing. Me," he paused again, "I don't understand the idea."

"I think Rudolph is convincing me that mankind is stupid," Daryl joked. "Try another question."

"What is love?"

Silence followed.

Daryl looked at his little brother and said, "Why couldn't you just have had grabbed that damn TV on the way to the car that day? The bear never really attacked us.

We could be blissfully frying bacon over the fire right now, not answering tough questions."

"I ask tough question?" Rudolph inquired.

"The toughest," Tim answered.

"When you mate with the female sasquatches, do you like them? I mean them personally, not just the sex part."

"The sex part?" Rudolph asked.

"Your turn, little brother."

Tim frowned and then said, "The sex part is the part that feels good when you mate."

"Yes. I know now. Like that part, but does not last long enough," the giant answered.

"Now he sounds like every female we've ever met," Daryl quipped.

"Speak for yourself, dude. I've never had any complaints," Tim bragged.

Daryl rolled his eyes.

Tim continued with their new friend, "Beyond that good feeling, that doesn't last long, do you like them? Do you wish you could stick around and be friends?"

"No. After good feeling, they hit and bite until I leave."

"But do you wish you could stay?" Tim prompted.

"No. They are horrible after mating."

Tim was getting frustrated, "But if they weren't horrible, would you want to stay?"

"No. Why would me? Whoops. Why would I?" he corrected himself. He was really trying.

Daryl spoke, "Maybe his kind can't feel love."

"No. I don't think that is it. He wants friends, now that he has discovered language. Language is a part of socialization. Maybe he is now capable, but has to learn about it."

"Me learn. Please. What is love? TV box people, when not being bad to each other, always loving. Touching faces. Squeezing each other. It looks nice."

Daryl took a stab, "There are many kinds of love. There is love between a male and a female that you mate with. There is love between friends, like us. Love between brothers. Tim and I are brothers. Do you know what brothers are?"

"Same birther?"

"Birther?" Tim asked, confused.

"Yes. He used that term before. Mother, not birther," Daryl taught him.

"Mother," the sasquatch repeated.

"Yes. I love him," Daryl said, pointing to Tim, "because he is my brother. We share the same mother. We love our mother. We have a pet dog, and we love him. His name is Roscoe."

"You mate? All of you?"

"No. Only with special females. Girl humans," Daryl said, finding his own ability to describe love inadequate.

"Marriage female. TV box show me The Bachelor. You give a rose flower and then mate," Rudolph said, displaying his limited understanding of man's ridiculous perversion of true love.

"Rudolph, let us get you a dog. That would be a good start. Meet us back here in two days. Two moon and suns, or however you mark time," Tim requested.

"Me," he pause, "I understand."

The beast left, and the brothers packed up camp.

The drive out was interesting.

Channel 7

"What is love? Holy shit! I now officially know that I don't know what love is," Daryl whined.

"Same here. I'm still with Gail, and I don't think I love her. I'm the last person that should be teaching anyone, or anything, about love."

"You just like the mating part, don't you?" Daryl joked.

"Truth be told, I don't even like that anymore. I feel like I'm using her, and that makes what we are doing wrong. I need to break it off."

"So, do it. Before her brother gets ordained on the internet and marries you two without you knowing it," Daryl warned.

"Without me knowing it? You, sir, are an idiot," Tim declared.

"I'm an idiot? I'm not the one living with a woman I don't care about."

There was a moment of silence. Daryl knew he hurt Tim's feelings.

"Back to Rudolph," Daryl changed the topic back to the task at hand. "How are we going to answer his question? I think it could be important in his continued development."

"You serious? Why is his continued development our responsibility at all?" Tim asked.

"Because you took your damn solar powered TV into the woods and lost it!"

"I didn't lose it! Giant Rudolph stole it!" Tim insisted.

"Either way, you brought it. And now we have a talking sasquatch who wants to learn about life as we know it. That is on you, brother. If we ignore him, he'll try to make contact with someone else and get himself captured or killed. We can't let that happen."

"You are such a Boy Scout. Fine! Let's get him a dog! If there is anything that can teach him to feel love, it's a dog," the younger brother declared.

The plan was set.

Rudolph sat watching the TV. More news. A car accident killed two children. Rudolph felt sad.

The next story told about a man who shot three people where he used to work. He had been fired, whatever that meant. One of his coworkers died from his wounds. Rudolph wasn't sure how to feel.

A hospital, where sick and injured humans went, had caught on fire. The pictures showed big, red trucks with colorful lights. He liked those.

And the next major story was about a woman who had stolen money from an elderly couple and was caught by the couple's daughter. Rudolph didn't really understand ownership and stealing property. He concluded that humans were territorial about their possessions.

The final story was about a little boy singing at a senior home. Humans put their older people in herds with other old people. He had seen it on other programming over the last few years. Entire packs of old people stuck together. It didn't seem like a good plan to keep so many together. They were easy prey.

The next show was, 'I Love Lucy.' He thought it made more sense to love Lucy than Raymond. She made big faces and unusual noises. While he watched her, he caught himself smiling involuntarily. He had yet to actually laugh, but he was working up to it.

'Criminal Minds' followed and it made Rudolph wonder what kind of monsters humans really were.

Eventually, its charge ran down. The time it was able to run was getting shorter and shorter as the solar batteries were beginning to fail.

Rudolph thought about Daryl and Tim. He did not see them as a threat. They were kind, as far as he understood the term.

They were going to get him a dog. He knew from TV that dogs were supposed to be good friends. Man's best friend, but he wasn't a man.

The next day, the brothers went to the pound. They weren't sure getting a puppy was a good idea. They didn't want Rudolph seeing it as an hors d'oeuvre.

There were several large dogs. They chose a three-year-old black Labrador named Nick. He was a bundle of energy, which is why his owners gave him up for adoption. Tim couldn't imagine Nick in a home with nice things.

Outside of being a bit rambunctious, Nick was a sweet dog. He would be a perfect companion for Rudolph, but there was a fear that maybe Nick would reject Rudolph out of fear, or possibly a natural dislike for his species.

Rudolph put off an odor that was capable of turning heads. His breath was not very pleasant either. The dog may either love the smells or take umbrage. They would find out soon enough.

After having custody of Nick for three days, they headed out into Rothrock State Forest. The three days showed that Nick was not overly housebroken. They cleaned up after his mistakes, but knew in the forest it wouldn't matter.

It had lightly snowed, which made their drive a little slower than usual. Once at their spot, they parked and left Nick in the car.

They stood at their usual encampment, cupped their hands together to act as megaphones and yelled, "RUDOLPH!" several times.

After waiting in silence for about five minutes, they repeated the calls. Once again, they waited for Rudolph to respond.

Rudolph may have been asleep or possibly in another area of the forest. Tim tried one more thing. He returned to the Cherokee and beeped the horn in staccato fashion.

Twenty minutes had passed when Rudolph finally stepped into the clearing where they were waiting.

The beast looked at them and let loose with a loud, "Good morning, Vietnam!"

The brothers looked at each other, a bit bewildered.

"Robin Williams," Rudolph said, and then, "What is a Vietnam?"

"It's a country," Tim answered.

"What is a country?" the sasquatch asked.

Daryl shook his head and said, "Another concept we take for granted. Counties, states and countries. He doesn't understand boundaries or borders. Or governments, for that matter."

"Rudolph, you have a lot to learn. Almost too much to learn," Tim said sadly.

"TV watch, less and less. It goes dark quicker than when I start watching," he told them.

"The solar battery is failing. We need to get him a new solar TV. Otherwise, his learning will come to a halt," Daryl said.

"I've been thinking. Maybe that isn't a bad thing," Tim remarked. "What good will come from this continuing?"

Daryl was shocked at first. To him, meeting Rudolph was the most miraculous thing he had ever witnessed. A myth comes to life and on top of that, it talks. Probably the only one of his kind that talks.

To the older of the two men, it wasn't like lightning striking the same place twice, it was like lightning striking the same place ten times. This would never happen again, and Tim was treating it like a bad thing.

But then the older sibling fast forwarded in his mind to where this was going. Rudolph didn't understand so many things that humans take an entire childhood to learn. A childhood of going to school every day.

Numbers, colors, geography, biology, math, history, chemistry and physics. These things were learned in stages and steps, and they certainly didn't have time to teach them.

And did the big man/animal understand humor, sarcasm, make believe or the difference of opinions between people on so many subjects? These things took time to learn, and some humans struggled with them.

He had picked up the basic language, but how much of what he saw on television did he understand? And how much was his mind poisoned by shows that were purposely provocative?

In what seemed like a long time, but was actually only moments, Daryl understood his brother's question much better than he wanted to. The more Rudolph learned, the more he would be at risk of being unhappy, misunderstood and unfulfilled.

In this case, the term *ignorance is bliss* might be the truest example that Daryl had ever seen.

"Why did you go silent on me?" Tim asked.

"Just thinking about your question. Are we screwing up?"

"What this means, screwing up?" Rudolph asked.

Just then a muffled bark came from the Cherokee. The two brothers had temporarily forgotten about Nick and their grand experiment in love and companionship.

Daryl went and retrieved the dog. Nick hopped out of the car, wagging his tail a mile a minute. He was glad to be freed.

They walked back to Tim and Rudolph.

Nick's ears went back. His tail stopped wagging, and it stiffened straight out behind him. He began to growl.

Rudolph began to growl as well.

Tim touched Rudolph's shoulder, "Stop growling. Be kind to him. His name is Nick, and he needs you to be nice. He's not as smart as you," Tim explained.

Nick wasn't on a leash and could bolt at any moment. Tim and Daryl stood by Rudolph and tried coaxing him to come.

Nick held his head down and inched forward. There was still a rumbling noise coming from the dog's throat. He was unsure what was happening or what to expect.

Tim got down on his haunches and held his left hand out, while stroking Rudolph's leg with his right hand. Soon, Tim found himself petting Nick and Rudolph. The dog was slowly closing the gap.

"Talk to him, Rudolph, so he sees you're human," Daryl said, and immediately realized the absurdity of the words he had just spoken.

Rudolph bent down, "Hello, Nick. I Rudolph. I Rudolph, Nick."

Tim started to open his mouth to correct Rudolph's grammar and Daryl cut him off, "If you correct him, I swear I'll kick you in the head." Tim remained silent.

"I, Rudolph and want friend. Be my friend, Nick."

If a dog could possibly look confused, Nick was displaying the emotion as he inched forward. A few moments passed, and Rudolph touched Nick's head.

"Be gentle," Tim warned. "Soft touches. Do you know soft?"

"Yes. Like Charmin bathroom tissue. Soft," Rudolph repeated.

Daryl snorted at the commercial reference. There was another thing. Did Rudolph understand toilet paper commercials? Or even for what a toilet would be used? So much had to be going over his head as he watched the TV.

Commercials for Swiffer WetJet mops and Dyson vaccuums couldn't be making sense to him. Rudolph didn't clean the floor of his cave. And how long would it be before he asked either himself or Tim what Viagra was used for?

What did he think of talking M&Ms or the guy with the emu in the insurance commercial? And he couldn't possibly care less about Ford tough or finger lickin' good chicken or how great Frosted Flakes are. Do the Dew? America runs on Dunkin? This was maddening to think of how much the poor beast would never understand.

This experiment with Nick had to work. At least they could walk away, knowing they had helped Rudolph find a friend.

Rudolph was petting Nick gently. The dog's tail was starting to wag. Rudolph got down on his knees. Nick jumped up to lick his face. It was working.

Suddenly, Daryl was flooded with new worries.

Would Rudolph be able to take care of a dog? Dogs needed to be fed. They needed attention. He and his brother may have assumed too much.

He watched as the dog and the sasquatch were forming a bond. It was as if Nick knew that this was his new master and friend. The canine was paying attention to Rudolph, almost exclusively, leaving Tim and Daryl out in the proverbial cold. It was good.

"Rudolph, Nick needs to be fed. Do you know what I mean? He needs food and water every day. You can't ignore him, or he'll die or run away. Do you understand? You must take care of him and protect him. He is your pet."

Rudolph stood up. And smiled. It was a real smile.

"I take good care of my Nick. Food and water. I understand. I share my food with my Nick."

Daryl and Tim thought it was great how Rudolph was using the possessive adjective *my,* when referring to the dog.

"Rudolph, we'll come back in a few days to check on you guys. Here is a twenty-five-pound bag of dog food. Here are two bowls. Put water in one bowl and fill it when it is empty. Put his food in the other bowl. He can also eat what you eat. Okay?" Daryl instructed.

"Me understand," Rudolph said, and then looked sheepishly at Tim because he knew he had said it wrong.

The brothers left.

Channel 8

The weather became increasingly cold as November moved towards Thanksgiving. The Thursday holiday was always followed by the Monday deer season.

The brothers had visited Rudolph and Nick at least once a week since the middle of October. They brought dog food, a dog bed and several blankets.

The sasquatch and his dog were doing wonderfully. The brothers loved seeing them together. Nick rarely left Rudolph's side. Rudolph petted the dog gently and every now and again, the huge beast would rub his forehead against the dog's forehead. Nick seemed to love it, and it was a most endearing sight.

After a few weeks, Daryl declared, "Rudolph has learned to love another creature. That's huge, Tim!"

Tim, holding back tears, agreed. It was better than any contrived Hallmark movie. This was a being that had never loved before, finding the capacity to love. It raised a new question for Tim, whom had finally broken up with Gail.

His break up had led him to spend some counseling time with his pastor. Being free of her made him feel closer to God. The guilt of their relationship was gone.

Daryl had insisted that Tim never really had anything to feel guilty about, but he didn't truly understand how long Tim had used the woman, misleading her, because he didn't have the backbone to cut bait. The deception was the reason for his guilt, not the so-called living in sin.

Now, feeling more strongly connected to his faith, he wondered about Rudolph. He questioned whether the creature had a soul. Learning socialization and loving, similar to a human, seemed to blur the line of who or what the creature really was.

If he and Daryl had brought this creature to this point because of the TV and their continued meddling, were they responsible for the beast's afterlife? Or was an afterlife never in the cards?

Rudolph was becoming so human. Was he a throwback to an earlier form of humanity? Tim hated thinking these thoughts. And besides Daryl, there was no one he could talk to. He began including Rudolph in his prayers. He hated the burden.

Two days after deer season had begun, they drove to Rothrock to see Rudolph. They wore the requisite bright neon orange knit hat and safety vests. Getting shot was the last thing they wanted.

Daryl parked the car. They got out and began calling Rudolph and Nick's names.

They waited twenty minutes and began calling again.

Five minutes later, Nick showed up, alone. He was agitated and barking and kept running into the woods and then coming back to bark at the men.

Daryl looked at Tim and said, "If he were Lassie, I'd say that Timmy had fallen into a well, and we are supposed to follow."

Tim replied, "Let's go!"

The men followed Nick. The rambunctious dog kept getting way ahead of them, and then having to run back to them and barking excitedly.

They finally arrived at a large rock formation.

"Look!" Daryl said, pointing. "Looks like a large cave entrance." The dog popped out and barked at them.

"Must be the place," Tim remarked.

Both men entered the cave, filled with dread.

Using their cellphone flashlights, they found Rudolph, leaning in a heap against the wall of the cave. His breathing was raspy, when he breathed at all.

"Look, Tim! There's blood in the middle of his chest."

Looking more closely, the blood had run down his front and pooled between Rudolph's legs.

"Rudolph, it's Daryl and Tim. Hey, buddy, can you hear us?" Daryl asked.

Rudolph's eyes opened.

The giant gasped, "Nick, needs food! Feed Nick. Needs water."

Tim felt the tears start to flow. Rudolph was in dire shape, and he was worried about Nick. If there had been any doubt before, there was none now. Rudolph had learned to love.

Daryl grabbed his own canteen and filled the dog's water bowl. Tim found one of the bags of dog food and filled Nick's food bowl.

Nick had no interest in either. He was lying down beside Rudolph, with his head on his paws and quietly whining.

Rudolph rasped, "Me die now. No tomorrow. No more love. Take Nick."

"You did really good with Nick, buddy. You loved him really well. And he obviously loves you," Tim told him.

"Love Nick. Please…" Rudolph sighed and his head fell forward.

Daryl shook his shoulder and yelled, "Rudolph! Rudolph!" He was gone.

The two brothers sat cross legged across from their dead friend and cried. There was no pretense of machismo. They wept. There was truly no other option to express their emotion.

Rudolph's demise was due to a hunter's bullet. It was the only explanation that made sense.

After they had exhausted their tears, Daryl asked Tim, "Do you still want your solar TV back?"

"No. We'll bury it with him."

"Bury? That is going to be some hole. We don't have shovels," Daryl reminded his brother.

"Don't need shovels. Take me home. I have a secret. We just need to go get it and come back."

They tried desperately to get Nick to come with them. He wouldn't budge. Nick needed time to let go. They could get him when they came back.

Their round trip took two hours and twenty minutes.

Once again, they stood at the entrance to the cave.

"Okay, little brother. What did we just pick up? What is in your bag?"

"Well, as you know, I work at construction sites. Over the years, I have come into possession of leftover materials. And in this bag are three sticks of dynamite. I have been wanting to get them out of the house. And now I know why I kept them. This is how we will bury Rudolph."

The first job was to remove Nick from the cave. Tim had what was needed for that as well. They removed his bowls, the dog bed and blankets.

Then Tim coaxed Nick out of the cave with a hot dog. Once out, Daryl put a collar on Nick and then hooked up a leash.

Tim entered the cave and prepared the dynamite for detonation. Using a one-hundred-foot fuse, he lit a match and then the brothers and Nick quickly headed away from the cave. Nick had to be coerced with an additional hot dog.

The explosion was somewhat muffled by the thick rock of the cave. Smoke and dust ejected out from the cave opening.

The brothers stared at the large rock formation. A large crack was heard and then, as ifß in slow motion, the rocks collapsed in on themselves.

Rudolph was officially buried.

Having learned to love, Rudolph had become human. Or maybe, but for a few circumstances, he had been human all along.

The Child

Toddler and The Sasquatch 1

Loraine was talking on her cellphone with her sister, Pam. She should have been paying attention to her son.

He was kicking a ball. At three years and two months, he still lacked the coordination to kick it with any gusto. But once in a while, in between falling down, he got lucky.

The ball headed towards the street. It was very sparsely traveled. The forest started across from their front yard and very few houses shared the street as part of their address.

The ball entered the roadway, and just as Cody stepped into the street to go after it, Loraine screamed, "No, Cody! STOP!"

He ended up in the middle of the road. He stopped and looked at his mom like she was crazy. She ran out and swooped him up in her arms and returned him to their yard.

She scolded him for going into the roadway and threw the ball closer to the house and said, "Kick it closer to home, sweetheart."

She then rejoined her conversation with Pam, leaving the boy frustrated and confused. He began the playful kicking all over again, slowly edging towards the road just as before.

She watched from behind the trees across the road. This season her womb had been left barren. She had only mated once, and it had not resulted in a pregnancy.

Her last child had been stillborn and that was two years ago. The yearning within her to love and nurture a child was overwhelming her.

The smooth, hairless child across the street was a bit repulsive, but it was still a child that she knew she could love. The smooth-skinned mother hardly paid any attention to it.

The female sasquatch's yearning to be needed was pushing her to the brink of a decision. Her not so primitive mind was working overtime.

She continued her vigil.

Forty-five minutes after the road incident, Peter pulled his truck into the driveway. There was Cody, sitting next to the garden, eating dirt. *And there's my damn wife,* he thought, *yacking on her cellphone, most likely with Pam.*

He hated his sister-in-law. She was the older of the two sisters. A bigger busybody could not be found. She was a rumor monger and gossiper of the highest order. And she was turning Loraine into a junior version of herself. Yes, he hated her and her negative influence on his wife.

He was beginning to resent Loraine as well. It didn't start out this way. When they were first dating, he barely knew she had a sister. Everything was about Peter and Loraine, as it should have been.

After they married, Pam began inserting herself into the relationship. Once Cody was born, Pam became Loraine's go to expert on everything child related. As her relation with her sister grew closer, she and Peter grew farther apart.

He didn't marry Pam, but she was a big part of his marital relationship, and he feared it was going to lead to a split. If it weren't for Cody, he might have already pulled that trigger.

It was 5:17 p.m. and he would have appreciated a hot dinner waiting on the table when he arrived home. After all, she was home all day, and he had been working at the mill. He was exhausted.

He got out of his truck to go rescue his son, before he ate a bug or something worse. Picking the boy up, he kissed his forehead and began gently wiping away the dirt from around his mouth.

He heard Loraine say, "Gotta go. Peter's home. Yes, as usual. Bye bye."

"Hello. How was work?" she asked.

"Tiring and boring. How was talking on the phone all day? I'm sure there's a hot, delicious meal waiting for me inside, right?" He said more sarcastically than he had intended.

She looked hurt. He didn't care.

"I did laundry today and the grocery shopping, if you must know," she answered a bit testily.

He couldn't stop himself, "Did our son eat anything today? I mean besides dirt, Loraine."

"Screw you!" she shouted.

"That would be a first in quite a while too," he answered. Their physical relationship had fallen away to almost nothing.

She looked at him and said, "Come on then. I'll lay on the bed and let you have your way, but don't expect anything other than that."

"Good Lord! How would that be any different than the last time? Or the time before that?"

"If you are so unhappy, why do you stay?" she asked angrily.

"I'm holding the answer to that question. Look at us. You let your sister do this to us. I hope you're both happy."

"Give me my son!" she grabbed Cody away from him.

He stood, watching her go into the house with Cody. He turned, walked back to his truck and got in. He sat fuming for a few minutes and then took off.

Peter headed to a little pizza restaurant that he liked. He could at least get a decent meal there and not have to look at her.

Inside the house, Loraine started supper. She put a frozen family-sized meat pie in the oven.

She admitted to herself for the first time that he was right. Pam had become more important to her than her husband, and maybe even her son.

"What the hell is wrong with me?" she asked herself aloud. She used to cook wonderful meals and enjoyed doing it, until Pam told her she wasn't some man's short-order cook.

They used to make love two or three times a week, until Pam convinced her that she was being treated like a whore.

She used to dote over Cody every minute of the day, until Pam told her she wasn't a nursemaid and that a child needed to become independent.

The problem was Pam. She needed to tell Cody she was sorry. She stepped out onto the front stoop to talk to him.

His truck was gone. She began to panic. Had she already let things go too far?

Her husband was a good man, a hard worker, a good provider and he had always treated Loraine with tenderness, until recently. He became more easily angered and quite put out by her inattentiveness to both him and his son.

She knew all this, and she knew it was wrong. But it was like she couldn't stop herself. She had developed some kind of weird dependency upon her sister.

She knew it had to stop. It seemed like she was watching a soap opera of someone else's life as it fell apart, but it was her own.

Her telephone rang. It was Pam. She let it go to voicemail. She then dialed her husband's number. He didn't pick up. Why should he?

He saw her name come up on his phone screen. His hand moved towards the phone, but he willed himself to stop. *Let her stew for a while, if she even cares*, he thought.

The pizza waitress was hitting on him. He played along. He wouldn't let it go too far. Peter wasn't that kind of man.

He knew that cheating on his wife was also cheating on his kid.

He couldn't believe how bad things had gotten.

Toddler and The Sasquatch 2

Peter made it home and slept on the couch. He awoke, brushed his teeth and left for work earlier than usual, before Loraine got out of bed.

He usually left before his wife awoke. She may not think anything of it. Peter didn't want to take any chances. Facing her this morning was the last thing he wanted.

On the way to work, his cellphone rang. It was her. He felt he could handle a phone call.

Loraine awoke earlier than usual. She noted that Peter hadn't come to bed. She got up and went into the living room and found a folded blanket on the couch. She had to stop this somehow.

She tried his cellphone. Surprisingly, he answered.

"Peter, let me speak. I have been foolish. Things have gotten out of hand. I'm sorry. Come home tonight and I will have a wonderful meal waiting. Then we can talk. Okay?"

"That sounds good, but unless you are ready to tell Pam to get lost, there's no point. She has changed you and ruined the good thing we had, and you let her do that. She has to go, or I need to go."

Silence.

Loraine agreed with him, but she didn't like being given an ultimatum. She felt her anger rising, but that was the last thing she needed. She fought it.

"I agree with you, Peter. We need to get us back on track. Pam has to stop her meddling. Just come home tonight with a positive attitude. I'll talk to Pam, I promise."

The call ended. Loraine felt hopeful.

She watched from her spot among the trees. She yearned to see the smooth child. Patience was something she had learned out of necessity, many years ago.

The smooth man had left a little earlier than his usual time. It wouldn't be long before the smooth woman and the child would emerge.

The mother would be talking into her hand most of the time, not paying attention to the child. The female sasquatch, obviously, did not understand what a cellphone was or the concept of remote communication. The closest that sasquatches came were their screams and tree trunk pounding.

The child should always be protected, she thought. The smooth ones were so strange. A child is always the top priority. Always.

Her yearning desire for a child was strong enough. It became greater, once she identified the smooth child as needing to be rescued from an uncaring mother.

The goal was now established.

Loraine was having a heated discussion with her sister. She had told her sister to stop trying to ruin her marriage and pay attention to her own life.

Pam was married to Ron. He was a high school biology and chemistry teacher. There were rumors about him and a certain English teacher. It was a small town, and secrets were difficult to keep.

Pam was livid that her little sister had done such an about face in their relationship. She asked Loraine how she could flip-flop so quickly. And then she blamed Peter.

"No, Loraine! Peter had nothing to do with this. I have been feeling manipulated by your constant suggestions and your criticisms. And now, I have hurt my husband. That never should have happened."

Pam was tenacious in explaining herself and defending her own marriage. The call was lasting longer than it should.

Cody was playing with his dump truck in the garden. Cody loved the dirt. While playing, he saw a squirrel. It darted back and forth and disappeared around the corner of the house. The toddler followed.

The separation between mother and child was perfect. The female sasquatch was capable of critical thinking. She watched as the mother turned her back while yelling into her hand.

The beast crossed the street and headed directly for Cody. The little boy never saw the beast coming. It swooped him up. He screamed, not because he was in pain, but because a huge, smelly beast was kidnapping him. He wanted his mommy.

"I can't see Cody, Pam. I've got to go!" Loraine said. She ended the call, and then she heard Cody scream. A cold hardness immediately developed in the pit of her stomach. A mother should never lose track of her son. *What is wrong with me?* she thought. She ran towards the corner of the house.

She stopped cold as she saw a huge monster holding her child. The thing crouched slightly and screamed toward her. She had never heard anything like it before.

She wasn't sure what to do, but it had Cody. Loraine ran forward, screaming back at the beast. In turn, the giant stepped forward, backhanded her and sent her sprawling.

It ran past her, crossed the street and bounded into the forest, holding on tightly to the little boy who had never stopped screaming.

Loraine lie face down and moaning. The swat she received from the beast was forceful and knocked the wind out of her. She was cognizant of the beast's movements, as she lie there gasping for breath. Loraine turned her head just in time to see the monster enter the forest.

Finally able to get to her feet, she crossed the street shouting Cody's name. She realized she needed help to get her son back. She immediately called Peter.

"Let me get this straight. A bigfoot came and snatched our son. You were talking to Pam and lost track of him and a monster from the forest took our baby. My God! What is wrong with you? Call the Sheriff's office! If he walked away, we need to get searchers looking for him!"

"Peter, he didn't walk away! He was kidnapped by a sasquatch! I'm telling the truth! Please believe me!" she pleaded.

"You know what, Loraine? I'll take over from here! I'll call the police! You just go and talk to your damn sister!" He ended the call. He momentarily wished for an old phone so he could slam it down into its cradle.

He called the Sheriff's department and sent them to his house. He told his boss that he had a family emergency, and then he headed to his home.

His mind was racing wildly. Had she really let their son wander off into the woods and now tried to cover it up with this preposterous story about a bigfoot?

Nineteen minutes later, he pulled into his own front yard, because the cops had already used up his driveway spaces. He got out and was confronted by a deputy sheriff, "Sir, you can't park here."

"It's my yard, and I'll do what I damn well please! Who is in charge?"

Loraine broke free from a group of people, which included her sister. She was crying and ran over to Peter and tried to hug him. He pushed her away. Peter had already made up his mind that his wife was a pathetic liar. As far as he was concerned, the marriage was over, and he just wanted Cody to be found safe and sound. That was job one.

Loraine cried, "It is all true, Peter! A monster took our boy! Please believe me!"

A sergeant from the Sheriff's department was in charge. His name was Porter. He grabbed Peter and steered him away from everyone else.

"I am having a hard time swallowing your wife's explanation, but she has been roughed up a bit. She has a swollen lip and a welt on her cheek. Something here," Porter told him.

He looked at the sergeant, "She could have done that to herself. She has a history of ignoring our son while she hangs on the phone for hours with her damn sister. Cody walked away. Neglect is the only explanation here. What are you guys doing about it?"

"A group of searchers is gathering at the firehall. They'll be here soon, and we will blanket these woods. But I need to ask you some questions," Sergeant Porter insisted.

"Go ahead, but make it quick. I want to find my son."

"When we got here, your wife was a wreck. Besides her physical injuries, she was crying and almost hysterical. It seemed genuine. When we asked about you, everything she said was complimentary and loving, but you pull in here acting like you hate the woman. Would you like to explain?"

Peter sighed, "I don't hate the woman, but we have serious marital problems because of her sister and other things. She told me she had come to her senses, just this morning.

"She was going to give her sister the heave ho and get our marriage back on track. But the first person I see her standing with over there was her sister, the first-class meddling bitch!

"So I believe she was on the phone with her sister and Cody walked away. She needed a fantastic lie to cover over her neglect. So now we are dealing with bigfoot. There. That's it," Peter concluded.

"If she needed a fantastic story, why not just say a man or woman came and stole the boy? Why would she concoct an unbelievable scenario? There is no reason to go that far overboard," Porter pointed out.

"She's desperate and just wasn't thinking straight, would be my guess. Just find my kid, please. I don't care if she claims alien abduction. My kid has to be in those woods. Start your search!"

"We already have men in there. A dog team is coming as well. If he's in those woods, we'll find him," Porter promised.

Loraine approached Peter once more. She grabbed his left arm with both hands and yanked him hard to get his attention, "You listen to me! Look into my eyes. I have never lied to you. Ever! A big beast grabbed Cody. I am smart enough to make up a better story, and you know it. You think I'm covering up because I ignored him, but I didn't!

"I was telling Pam to butt out of our lives, and he walked around the house. I immediately hung up with her and went to retrieve him and the monster was already there, holding him. I charged toward it to get our son, and it swatted me away like I was nothing. Look at my face! Look, damn you!"

Peter did look. The injuries were real. Her lip was cut and a bump had been raised on her right cheek. She certainly seemed sincere.

"Loraine, a bigfoot? Really? The cops don't even believe you," he told her.

"If you go in those woods to look for our boy, take your rifle. You'll need it," she warned him, and then she walked away.

Peter could only stare and wonder what was making her act this way. She wasn't backing down from the bigfoot story one bit.

Pickup trucks full of volunteers were showing up. Sergeant Porter began barking orders as they gathered in a group.

He explained to the men and women that they were looking for a little boy. Then he must have felt obligated to say it. He told them it may be an animal that abducted the child.

One of the men asked, "What kind of animal?"

There was a moment of silence and then Porter said, "Sasquatch."

Peter waited for them to start laughing. Not one of them did. All he heard was one man saying, "I'm glad we brought our rifles." Only then did Peter notice that several of the men and two of the women were holding guns.

Porter sent them out in groups of two, in a line covering about one hundred and fifty yards. They started on the road and walked into the woods.

Peter approached Porter, "They didn't laugh when you said sasquatch. And most of them are packing a rifle. What gives?"

"How long have you lived here?" Porter asked.

"About fifteen months," he answered.

"In this part of Washington, there are many who do not question anything where sasquatches are concerned. I think it's a bunch of hooey, but there are many who believe. As far as the rifles, there's plenty of bear and cougar on the loose. It is best to be armed when you go into the forest."

Peter looked over at Loraine. She was staring at him, to see what he was going to do. He headed into their house to get his rifle.

Toddler and The Sasquatch 3

Most of the volunteers were looking for a child. But a few were experienced woodsmen and were looking for any sign of a large animal.

Finally, one man yelled, "Need a sheriff's deputy over here!"

Corporal Gehlman was the nearest man. He ran over to see what the man had found that was so important.

"Look," the man began, "broken branches, hair from an unidentified animal and right there." The man was pointing at the ground. There lay a small, red and white sneaker.

Gehlman yelled, "Is Mr. Samson out here with us?"

Peter heard his name, "Over here!" he yelled back.

"Over here, sir!" Gehlman beckoned.

Peter Samson double timed over to the corporal. The policeman was holding Cody's sneaker, "Does this belong to your son?"

"Yes. That's Cody's shoe," Peter answered.

The man who had called the corporal over said, "It was right here. See this trampled brush and broken lower branches? And the animal hair right there and there." He pointed to two clumps hanging from the broken lower branches.

"Sasquatch?" Peter questioned.

"That would be my guess," the man said.

Peter thought of how he had treated Loraine, "Corporal, what do you think?"

"Don't quote me, because I'd deny it, but I agree with him. It looks like your wife's story holds water. Unofficially, of course," the Corporal emphasized.

Peter looked at the man who found the shoe, "Can somebody track the thing from here?"

"Not somebody, but something," the corporal said, "Look back at your house."

Peter looked and saw two women unloading two bloodhounds. The tracking dogs were getting leashed and were waiting for someone to give them instructions.

Corporal Gehlman ran back to Sergeant Porter and informed him of what they had found. The dogs and their handlers headed towards Peter.

The boy's father began to feel hopeful for the first time since learning of his son's disappearance.

The beast was moving quickly, considering its size. Her cave was just a little bit farther. She was feeling happy to have the child in her arms.

The same could not be said of Cody. He hadn't stopped crying since he was picked up. Unfortunately, they were far enough away from the searchers that his wailing could not be heard. He was no longer just scared. He was hungry as well.

The cave was just ahead. It was her sanctuary against a harsh world. Being alone did not suit her. Most sasquatches were loners, but not all.

There were all types of social situations among the mythical beasts. Even though most males and females stayed apart until mating season, there were females that grouped together for protection and socialization. Males sometimes did the same, and then there was the rare family group.

The family groups were headed by a dominant male, with as many as three females with juveniles. The juveniles were offspring of the dominant male. No others would be tolerated.

She would have loved a partner, male or female. Loneliness did not suit her and her existence was agony with no child to care for.

She had birthed eleven children over the years. They were the happiest times of her life. Gestation for the sasquatch was thirteen to fourteen months. Even when she had a child in her womb, she felt happy. It was another life to which she had connection.

Unfortunately for her, the children grew into adulthood and departed to find their own way in the forest. Every now and then, she would run into one of her offspring. There was remembrance, but no real tender moments.

She had mated with three of her sons over the years, but there was no tenderness there. Mating among the sasquatch was a ferocious affair. The females usually suffered bumps, bruises and sometimes a few bites.

This smooth child would give her some peace and purpose. Her loneliness was driving her mad. Now she would have companionship. She just wished it would stop crying.

Entering the cave did not improve Cody's mood.

The dogs sniffed the sneaker and then the hairs that had been collected. They were making quite a din. One handler, Sheila, said, "Wow! I haven't seen them this worked up in a long time. This is going to be a piece of cake."

With that, the dogs pulled their handlers deeper into the woods, followed by nine armed men and women, hoping for some action.

Corporal Gehlman and one other deputy accompanied the group. Gehlman gave orders for three other deputies to continue searching with the remaining volunteers. There was no guarantee that the dogs were going to be the final answer today. Corporal Gehlman suggested Peter stay behind with the searchers that were continuing closer to the house, just in case other evidence was gathered that needed identification.

Peter thought it was a bullshit move, but didn't want to interfere with the guys who knew what they were doing. He joined up with some other searchers along the search line.

Gehlman knew that once the dogs were on the scent, he didn't want to be babysitting the dad. These things could rapidly get dicey.

Sergeant Porter stayed at the house with Loraine and her sister. He and a few deputies had established a base camp there in the front yard.

He had the deputies keep the looky-loos from congregating. The road, which normally saw very little traffic, was becoming increasingly busy as word spread of the drama that was unfolding.

Additional volunteers were turned away. Having too many volunteers could do more harm than good. Many people show up at these events, not to be helpful, but to be nosy.

Sergeant Porter had experience in these matters. Living near Mount Rainier guaranteed it. Lost children, lost hunters, lost fishermen and lost vacationers were pretty regular occurrences.

Pam got Loraine alone and began trying to comfort her sister. She wasn't good at it.

"Loraine, Peter shouldn't have treated you like he did. You deserve better."

"Don't start," Loraine replied. "I can't blame him. I just told him our son was taken from us by a monster most people don't even believe exists. Don't talk badly about my husband!"

"I'm sorry. I can't stand to see you like this. He doesn't deserve you," Pam declared.

"No, Pam! You don't deserve me! I am worried sick about my son's welfare. You know, your nephew, Cody. But all you can do is talk about undermining my marriage. You are sick! Please leave!" Loraine requested, and then she walked away leaving her sister with her mouth agape.

Loraine stayed within earshot of Sergeant Porter. He was on his portable police radio receiving information from the searchers.

Pam returned to her car and left. She was angry. Loraine was right. Her nephew was missing, but she wasn't sure she believed Loraine's fantastic explanation.

If Loraine had neglected her son and he wandered off, why make up a story about a bigfoot? Pam thought she knew the answer. Loraine was afraid of Peter.

After the truth comes out, Loraine will be begging for her forgiveness. She could wait. She hoped her nephew survived the ordeal, for Loraine's sake.

Toddler and The Sasquatch 4

The smooth child had a foot covering on one foot but the other foot was bare. She wondered if that was important.

The female sasquatch realized that she knew very little about smooth children. She was smart enough to wonder whether smooth children and hairy children were different.

He had stopped crying. Sleep came for him because of exhaustion. She was grateful for the quiet time.

What do smooth children eat? she thought. Even though she was capable of critical thinking, she hadn't thought her plan through. She saw him eating dirt several times, but that didn't seem like a good thing to feed him.

While he slept, she needed to go get some meat for them both. That was her plan. Kill something fresh.

Then she heard the dogs, far off in the distance. She wasn't sure what that meant, but she was sure it wasn't good.

The two dogs, their handlers, nine searchers and two deputies traveled along the route that the female sasquatch had taken. The two female handlers kept telling the group that the dogs were giving great indications that they were locked onto something.

Having been told there was an animal involved, the handlers asked specifically what type of animal. They didn't want their dogs to get hurt. They had been told it was a sasquatch. That information excited both of them.

Their thinking was that if their dogs helped to find a bigfoot, it would be great publicity for their dog team. The downside, and there always is one, was that they weren't sure what a bigfoot could do to their dogs.

In truth, neither one believed in the creature, so they moved full steam ahead. They were pragmatists. They dealt with, and planned for, what they knew existed.

The dogs were barking up a storm. This search was going to end with them finding that for which they were looking. They were convinced of it, and in their minds, they would find the child.

It wasn't that they were wrong. But sometimes, being right was the last thing for which one should be hoping.

A game and wildlife officer showed up at the Samson home. His name was Warden Jonathan Littlewolf. He was a Native American, with family roots in the area that went back over three hundred years.

He was a friend of Sergeant Porter's. He had swung by to examine the hairs.

Loraine watched the two men closely. She saw the warden sniff the hair and jerk his head back sharply and then smile. Both began speaking in a very animated fashion.

The warden placed the hairs in a glassine envelope. Porter shook his hand, and then Warden Littlewolf left with the hairs.

Loraine approached Porter, "May I ask what the warden had to say? I saw him smell the hair and then take it with him."

"He is the only person who has ever had me half believing in sasquatches. He just confirmed that the hair that was found is most likely from one of the beasts. I'm still not saying I believe, but he certainly makes me want to give you the benefit of the doubt."

"Sergeant, I could have made up a dozen better stories than a sasquatch kidnapping my child. But I'm telling you that is what happened. But I have a notion, and you are not going to believe it," she told him.

"And what is that, Mrs. Samson?"

"I honestly don't believe she'll hurt him."

"She?" the policeman questioned.

"I'm just guessing, but the way she held him was more protective than anything else. It wasn't like she had just roughly snagged her next meal. She was cradling him."

"Ma'am. Let's hope you're right."

The dogs were getting closer, and she didn't know what she should do. Her first priority was to protect the child.

She stood ten yards from the cave entrance and waited. She had dealt with people's dogs before. It never ended well for the canines.

The two handlers were sisters. Adrianna and Carlotta Demitri had both earned bachelor degrees in Animal Behavior and Psychology from Utica College in Utica, New York.

They weren't twins, but they were only a year apart. Adrianna had been held back a year in preschool, which put the girls on the same educational and social trajectory. They loved it and had become best friends as well as sisters.

Both women were very attractive, but had shunned the dating scene to concentrate on working with their dogs, which so many men found off-putting. They found that men didn't like playing second fiddle or runner up to a dog.

Adrianna was twenty-nine and Carlotta was twenty-eight. They both had plenty of time to start a family, if they chose to do so. For now, it was all about the dogs and each other.

Carlotta was right behind Duke, which was her dog. Adrianna's dog was Maisy. Duke had the lead, which was typical during a search and rescue operation.

Carlotta noticed Duke becoming more agitated and Maisy becoming less vocal, almost subdued. She found it very unusual. Normally the dogs tried to outdo each other on the decibel meter.

Duke was straining at his leash. Carlotta was barely hanging on. He had never been this insistent, that she could remember. The kid must be really close.

Suddenly, there was nothing but slack. Carlotta looked down to see the leash attached to a broken collar. Duke was gone. Carlotta panicked and began running to catch up to her charge.

She came to a large, low rock formation and a clearing. She looked ahead in time to see a huge beast throw Duke against a tree. He yelped and then slid down the tree and came to rest at the base. He was not moving.

"Son of a bitch!" she yelled, while drawing her Glock 17. She crouched and took aim and fired. She hit her mark on the first shot, and the creature roared loudly. It was the kind of roar that those nearby can feel in their chest. It was scary.

She fired a second time, but missed. The beast had already moved, grabbed a large broken tree branch from the ground and was charging toward the dog handler.

Adrianna was trying to catch up to her sister, but Maisy was holding her back. They heard the yelp, the gunshot and the roar. Her dog had never cowered in the face of danger before. This was making Adrianna crazy, because she knew her sister needed her.

Luckily, the others in the group passed the older sister, and rushed to the aid of the other one. The first few, which included Corporal Gehlman, arrived to find Carlotta lying on the ground, unconscious and bleeding from the forehead.

The sasquatch was gone, but they could hear Cody wailing. Two men stopped to render first aid to the downed dog handler. Gehlman and a few others kept running, following the child's screams.

Adrianna finally got Maisy moving again and came upon the scene of her sister being helped to a sitting up position and taking a drink of water. She seemed like she was going to be okay.

The older sister then saw Duke. She looped Maisy's leash over a low branch on a nearby tree and went to check on him. He was unresponsive. She checked for a pulse. There was none. Duke was dead.

She walked back to where her sister was.

Carlotta looked up, "I'm okay. How is Duke?"

"You're not okay, so don't give me that crap! Just sit there and rest. As for Duke, I'm sorry sis, but he's gone."

The two men watched the exchange. As the sisters began crying, the men began feeling completely out of their element. They stood by and guarded the women, just in case the beast should return.

Gehlman, the other deputy, and the remaining seven men had the beast cornered against another group of large rocks. Gehlman had told them not to chance firing their weapons, for fear of hitting the boy.

The beast eyed them with contempt the entire time, while cradling the boy gently in her arms. Gehlman noticed its maternal demeanor.

He turned to the men, "She's trying to protect the boy. Look how she's holding him. She doesn't mean him any harm."

The others could clearly see that which Gehlman was referring. But Cody's loud protestations were making them nervous.

One man said, "It's a girl. She's got breasts, kind of."

And she did have breasts that were noticeable, even under the hair.

"Okay. So take it easy," Gehlman told them. "She grabbed a child and is now protecting it. So maybe this is a mother/child scenario of some sort."

The beast snarled at them.

Gehlman holstered his Glock 19. He then asked the men to lower their weapons. He knew he needed to keep everyone calm, including the sasquatch.

He had never believed before, but he had read enough to know that they were a form of man at some time in their development. At least that was one theory.

He stepped forward.

The creature hissed.

He spoke gently, "Now momma, we don't want to hurt you. We just want the child. His real mommy and daddy are worried."

The sasquatch cocked her head, as if listening.

He slowly took another two steps forward.

She inched backwards, holding the child away from him.

"Now momma, what are you going to feed that child? He can't eat what you eat. You're gonna make him sick. I know you don't want that."

One of the men said, "I can hit a squirrel at fifty yards with no scope. Why not just let me shoot her in the head?"

Gehlman turned and wasn't sure who said it, so he addressed the entire group, "I'm guessing she weighs six to seven hundred pounds. If she falls on him, it could kill the boy."

No one spoke again.

Gehlman returned his attention to the giant standing in front of him. He took three steps forward, while gently speaking to her, "Atta girl. I mean you no harm. We have to take care of that baby. Okay?"

She didn't move, but just stared at him.

Gehlman held his arms out, to show that he wanted Cody. He wanted her to know his intent. He wanted the child.

She looked at him as if she were in deep thought. He was getting through to her.

On some level, the female knew that taking the child was not acceptable behavior. She had reasoned that if she had a child and someone took it, that would be wrong.

She wasn't ready to give in. Gehlman got an idea. He radioed back to Sergeant Porter. He gave him their exact GPS coordinates.

Turning to the searchers, Gehlman said, "Relax gentlemen. We have to kill about half an hour or so."

He turned to the female giant and kept her busy, listening to him prattle on about nothing. She relaxed when she saw a few of the searchers lay down their weapons and sit cross legged on the ground.

The situation had taken on a new dimension. The searchers, whom had at first been terrified by the beast, were very quickly adjusting to the new reality and were taking cellphone pictures.

Gehlman's calm, levelheaded approach had affected everyone. The truth that was being witnessed was that besides the fact that she clocked Carlotta with a branch, the sasquatch meant no harm. The female sasquatch wasn't acting out in the same way a bear or a cougar would have.

The fact that she looked almost human was helping as well. Yes, she was big, but she wasn't flaunting that size advantage in any way.

One of the men said, "Corporal Gehlman, she's bleeding. The dog handler fired two shots. One must have hit the mark. Her left shoulder is bloody."

Gehlman hadn't noticed the sasquatch's wound until it was pointed out to him. *So much for having the trained eye of a cop*, he thought to himself.

He pointed to her shoulder, "Momma, you are hurt. Can I help you?"

She looked at her own shoulder and made a pouty face. It definitely hurt.

Gehlman thought that maybe helping her with her wound, after this was all over, would be a good start in paving the way for human/sasquatch relations.

It was just a thought, and he wasn't sure where it would end up. But finding the mythical creature to be real had to be the most momentous occasion in scientific history in quite a while. He was glad to be a part of it.

This one live creature could teach them more about man's ascent as the dominant species than anything in recent history. It may even have medical value, in the long run.

But for now, it was a waiting game.

Toddler and The Sasquatch 5

Sergeant Porter and two other deputies escorted Loraine and Peter to the coordinates that Gehlman had supplied. The couple came face to face with the beast.

Peter wanted to shoot it immediately and was restrained by Gehlman, "No, Mr. Samson! You might hit the boy!" Peter backed down.

Loraine was fascinated by the creature. She yearned to hold Cody, but had an eerie calmness where his safety was concerned, just as she had expressed earlier.

Gehlman took the lead, "Ma'am, I had you brought here to ask for your child back. One mother to another. We have determined that she's a female, and she has been so gentle with the boy. I've been calling her momma."

"Momma," Cody screamed when he saw his mother.

The female sasquatch's head whipped around when she heard him speak and then reach towards his mother. She watched him and was fascinated that he could speak or do anything other than cry and scream.

The female looked at Loraine with kindness.

Loraine spoke to her, "Momma, that's my boy. I need him back, please." Loraine could feel her emotions taking over. Tears began running down her cheeks, and Loraine wondered if the beast understood tears.

The female stared at Loraine for a full minute and then made a squeaky sound. Loraine dabbed at her tears with a Kleenex and saw a tear run down the beast's face. It was a connection.

Loraine could see the anguish in the female's face as more tears fell. Something more was going on and she expressed it, "This momma has lost a child. That is why she took Cody. She is hurting."

Peter said, "How do you know that?"

"I just do, honey. We have a connection in our pain. She didn't mean any harm. She just wants to stop hurting and grieving. She is like us."

Loraine talked loud enough for everyone to hear. The armed searchers were fascinated. They not only heard Loraine's words, but also saw the tears.

Loraine walked towards the beast. The big hominid did not move, posture or threaten in any way. Cody's mom was only three feet away. Cody was straining to reach her.

Loraine touched her. The animal positioned Cody so that Loraine could take him. She grabbed her son and said, "Thank you."

She turned to walk away, hugging her little boy. She was no more than seven feet away when four shots rang out. Everyone jumped, except the shooter.

Adrianna stood there, Glock 17 in hand and looking angry.

Loraine turned to see the momma sasquatch as she fell to her knees and then flop forward, face first. Two of the four shots were headshots.

Loraine handed Cody to Peter and ran back to the animal. Its head was turned, and she was looking up at Loraine. She grunted as the light and life drained from her eyes.

Loraine got down on her knees and put her hands on the beast's back and began sobbing. This was a true heartbreak unfolding in the forest.

Gehlman turned to Adrianna, "Why in the hell did you do that?"

"She hurt my sister and killed our dog! You got your kid back. It was time for her to die!"

Several of the men joined Loraine, at the creature's side. A few of them had tears in their eyes. The beast didn't deserve to die. If Loraine was correct, the beast had already suffered enough and had made a real connection with humans.

The animal's carcass was retrieved. Every news outlet in the world was carrying the story. Sasquatches were real.

Adrianna and her sister were interviewed over and over. Each time the story became more outlandish and the lonely, heartbroken sasquatch was portrayed as a blood thirsty fiend.

Adrianna took credit for killing the first of the previously thought to be mythical beasts. She made it sound like she had snatched Cody from the jaws of death, while everyone else just stood around whimpering.

It was summed up best by Sergeant Porter when he said to Corporal Gehlman, "Not all assholes are men."

The Hiker

Trailhead 1

Prisoner number 478923-2021 was on the loose. The Appalachians were a great place to hide. It was summer.

Daytime temps in the upper elevations were tolerable. There were creeks and streams everywhere. Potable water was not a problem.

Game was plentiful as well, if one had a rifle. He did not. His plan was to get a weapon. 478923-2021 knew that the mountains were filled with shacks and shanties used by the hill folk.

He came to a clearing that looked down into a valley. He saw several plumes of rising smoke that he presumed were from the house chimneys below. His plan was to follow the rising smoke and locate a home that he could ransack.

478923-2021 was a desperate man. In fact, he was a killer. He wasn't a psychopath. He knew right from wrong. He had a conscience, and he felt guilt and remorse.

But mostly, he felt anger. His childhood had been unbelievably screwed up.

His mother was a meth addict. She would trade sexual favors right on the street to earn money to support her habit. He learned early on not to trust in her for anything.

She was arrested by the cops many times, and he would hide until the police left. Other addicts made sure he had some food. Some abused him.

His mother eventually died on the streets, and he was placed in foster care. That was almost as bad as the streets. He endured more physical and mental abuse than sexual abuse.

He learned to hate people at a very early age.

478923-2021 found love at eighteen, working at a fast food burger joint. She was a young girl named Naomi. She was sweet and kind, and she felt sorry for him because he was so alone and living on the streets.

He had learned where he could bathe and where to find heat in the winter months. He stumbled into the job and saved every penny he could.

The burger joint was his main source of food. He worked hard for the owners, and he never stole from them. Eventually, Naomi's pity became love.

A year later, when he was nineteen and she was seventeen, he asked her to be his wife. She said yes, and they set up house in a one room, studio apartment. Most people would describe it as a dump, but it was their dump, and they loved it.

Fate can sometimes be capricious. They loved each other greatly, but could not conceive. It caused strain on their relationship, for both wanted children. But they could not afford to go to the doctor to get help.

Eventually, she blamed him for their inability to have children, and he blamed her barren womb on her. It drove them apart.

They began fighting and bickering daily. On one particularly cold Sunday in January, he was trying to watch football. She decided it was a good time to pick a fight.

So he killed her. He bashed her head in with a heavy ashtray, which they used as a candy dish, because neither of them smoked.

He sat, cradling her lifeless body in his arm for hours and cried. The train wreck which was his life continued.

Sentenced to thirty-five years in jail, he became even more bitter about his bad fortune. While in prison, he killed another inmate. He stabbed the man with a shiv over thirty times.

This unfortunate turn of events added fifty more years to his sentence. There would be no chance for parole. At age twenty-six, he was looking forward to a lifetime behind bars.

Escape, at any cost, now became his objective.

Five months after receiving the additional time, 478923-2021 was put on a highway work detail. During the lunch break, 478923-2021 asked for permission to urinate in the woods next to the road.

Two guards stayed with the other seven prisoners and one guard came with 478923-2021. After ten minutes in the woods, the prisoner got the drop on his guard. Once behind him, he forced the guard to his knees and then broke his neck.

He grabbed for the man's rifle, just as a bullet pinged off the tree beside him. One of the other guards had followed, thinking it was taking too long. 478923-2021 began running into the woods, empty handed.

The game was afoot. The guards quickly called for backup, an ambulance and search parties. Within thirty minutes, a State Police helicopter was in the air. Dog teams were assembled.

478923-2021 had become the most wanted man in Pennsylvania.

Zebulun was the patriarch of his clan. He was named after the sixth son of Jacob and Leah, from the Old Testament. The reason was simple, he was the sixth son of his mother and father. He was also the last.

His five siblings had passed on. All of them had died, relatively early in their lives. His brother, Ezekiel, had lived the longest, and he died at forty-two.

Mountain life was hard. It was even harder if you were foolish. And foolishness was the hallmark of the McNary clan. Unwashed and uneducated, they intermarried with cousins and an occasional kidnapped girl they would snatch off the Appalachian trail.

Those girls would usually last long enough to produce a child, which gave some new blood to the clan. And then they would escape, die of disease or would have to be killed because they were more trouble than they were worth.

Actually, only one had ever escaped. The McNarys had prepared for the law to come looking for them, but it never happened. Unbeknownst to the clan, the poor girl became lost and died of exposure. To the young girl, it was preferable to being a sex slave for the Appalachian hillbillies.

Zebulun had reached the ripe old age of sixty-two. He had two wives. His first was a cousin named Ruth, and the second was his first daughter, Esther. The tension within the household was so thick, you could cut it with the proverbial knife.

That tension was not an issue for Zeb. If the women disturbed him with what he called their *caterwauling,* he would beat one or both. They had learned quickly to keep their rivalry out of sight, although it would sometimes see the light of day and a beating would commence.

The McNarys numbered thirty-one. Zebulun ruled them with an iron fist. He was also the source of wisdom for the group, and no one challenged him. The clan had been thirty-three strong at one time in recent history. Those two additional McNarys had tried to assert their will on the group. Zeb killed them both in public fashion. It was a lesson for all to learn.

The hillbilly men hunted, fished, chopped firewood and built cabins. They built beautiful cabins. Zeb insisted on it. Their homes didn't have glass in the windows, electricity or indoor plumbing, but they were well-built structures. The cabins all contained wood carvings throughout.

Zeb was a woodcarver, and he taught the others the skill. Their cabins would have confused those who saw the shanties that the other clans in the mountains called home.

The McNary clan leader had actually worked for a man who built homes in Mount Holly Springs. Zeb was in his early twenties, and he wanted to see what was beyond the hills.

He helped to build beautiful homes for 'rich arseholes,' as he put it. After two years, he tired of being looked down upon for his lack of education and his less than stellar hygiene.

He returned to the hills and began teaching himself how to carve. One of his coworkers was a master at the craft and had tried to take him under his wing.

Zeb liked the man and actually respected him for his kindness and fantastic skill. Unfortunately, the man had a fourteen-year-old daughter, and as soon as Zeb started showing an interest, the relationship with the man ended.

To Zeb, a fourteen-year-old girl was fair game, and he didn't understand the sudden snub. It was actually the last straw, living among the 'fancies,' which is another term he used for people living in civilized society.

The yearning to carve came back to him, and he became a master in his own right. He taught others and soon the old cabins took on a new flair. Then the yearning to build new cabins with carved features throughout took hold.

Even the outhouses took on a fancy flair.

On this warm, summer day, the men went about hunting and fishing to feed the clan. The younger men chopped wood. The women boiled clothing and hung the garments out to dry. They polished their cabins' woodwork with a combination of corn oil, moonshine and beeswax that Zeb had developed.

And they also prepared themselves for the physical assault, which their husbands called sex. There were very few women in the hills of Pennsylvania that could claim sex was enjoyable. It was rough, and it was usually quick. The men walked away satisfied, and the women were a bit sore. It was what they had come to expect.

This was life in the McNary clan.

478923-2021 was following the plumes of smoke from the McNary fires. He was getting closer and could actually smell wood smoke carried on the light breeze that flowed through the forest.

He stopped and held his breath. A middle-aged man holding a rifle was coming his way. 478923-2021 was still wearing his orange prison jumper. He needed different clothes, but this greasy looking, dirty man was not with whom he wanted to exchange clothing.

But that rifle was exactly what he needed. His orange jumper would be his undoing. He decided to be bold.

He stepped out from behind the tree which he had taken cover. The escapee held his hands over his stomach and bent over. He began to moan, "Help me! I've been shot by a hunter!"

The hillbilly didn't recognize the jumper as prison issue, but instead it was the orange gear that the fancies wore when they entered the woods to hunt. His dimwitted mind saw an opportunity to make money. If he helped this man, there could be a reward. That is how he understood the outside world worked, always throwing their money around.

And if the man died before he could get help, he probably had a wallet on him. He would give the money to Zeb. Their leader would go into town sometimes and bring back things that they could use.

The hunters name was Enoch.

"Don't see no blood," he said to the man in orange. "Maybe it ain't so bad." He leaned in for a closer look.

478923-2021 stood up and jammed a pointy stick that he had been concealing in his sleeve into the man's throat. Blood gushed forth as if it needed to escape, or it would cease to exist.

The hillbilly staggered backwards and dropped his rifle. Blood ran down his dirty denim bib overalls. The murderer didn't mind. He had already decided he would not be using the filthy rags that the man wore.

The escaped prisoner stood over the hillbilly and watched the spark of life leave his eyes. He questioned why he had to kill the man. He could have overpowered him, unless he turned out to be one of those strong, wiry types. He convinced himself that he couldn't take that chance, but he actually felt bad. This was someone's son. Maybe he was a father and husband.

It scared 478923-2021 how much more easily it was becoming to take a life. He picked up the rifle. He then reached down and tore off a piece of denim from the dead man's overalls. He then employed the remnant to wipe blood off of the stock of the rifle.

The rifle was a Winchester .22. A quick check revealed the rifle held fifteen rounds in its tubular magazine. The rifle's new owner leaned over the dead man and rifled (no pun intended) through his pockets. The search yielded seventeen more rounds.

He shrugged. It was better than nothing. A .22 LR bullet wasn't the deadliest, but it would have to do.

Trailhead 2

Major Thomas Kincaid, of the Pennsylvania State Police, was heading up the search coordination. He was in charge of the prison units, sheriff's units, state policemen and policemen from local jurisdictions. One hundred and forty-eight individuals, five dogs and two helicopters were actively involved.

Over fifty percent of the Appalachians are owned by private individuals or companies that are designated as absentee owners. Over forty percent of the mountains are owned by companies who occupy or use the land. And lastly, eight percent of the land is owned by the United States government.

The federal government was on the sidelines as this search continued. Even the FBI had stepped aside to allow the Pennsylvania State Police to have jurisdictional control.

The FBI had most of their local resources tied up on a kidnapping with transportation across state lines. They were glad to sit this one out, unless requested.

There were some political underpinnings as well, which were tied to the private ownership of the land. The mountain crossed through fourteen states, and cooperation between states worked better when the federal government stayed out of the mix.

Kincaid kept only the dog teams in the field after dark. All others were recalled until daylight.

478923-2021 was proving to be elusive.

Zebulun was in a foul mood. Enoch hadn't returned. Now he had to make the decision to go look for him in the dark.

They roused Homer, the coonhound. Enoch's wife supplied an unwashed shirt, which were plentiful. The dog sniffed it and the dog, knowing what was expected, was off.

Zeb and three other men followed the hound. As far as hunting dogs went, Homer was a good one. He always treed his coon and anything else he was set upon.

In less than an hour, the men found Enoch's corpse. They used crank flashlights that lit up the area well with a bluish tinted light. It made Enoch's corpse look even more cold and lifeless.

Zeb stared down at his clansman and shook his head. His slow witted second in command, Joshua, said, "Poor feller. Must have fell on that stick at just the right way to do that."

"Oh, yeah," Zeb began, "and then I guess his rifle got up and ran away by itself. Do you think that's how it happened, Josh?"

While Zeb and his clansmen were finding their murdered friend, 478923-2021 had found their village. He was surprised at the quality of their cabins. Even in the dark, he could tell they were more than shanties and shacks.

At first there was no one moving about outside. Then he saw movement. It was a young girl of about thirteen or fourteen. She wore a gunny sack dress, no shoes and had long, stringy looking hair.

The girl was tending a fire in the middle of their hamlet. Its purpose was to guide the searchers back home. The escaped prisoner had no clue as to its purpose.

All the vile man could think was that he hadn't had access to a woman for several years. As the girl melted into the darkness to gather more wood, he struck.

He grabbed her around the waist with his right arm and held his left hand over her mouth. He dragged her into the forest.

She smelled unclean, but he just needed a few minutes. His efforts were made all the easier because she wore no undergarments.

She struggled, trying desperately to get away, which just made him all the more excited. He was through with her in no time at all.

He whispered, "If you make a sound, I'll kill you."

She understood and just lay there staring up at him.

He didn't kill her, which made him feel good that he fought that urge and won. He slowly backed away from her, while telling her to count to one hundred before getting up.

478923-2021 had no clue that the girl had problems counting beyond twenty. Once the girl ran out of fingers and toes, she was lost.

The escaped prisoner heard men's voices. He stuck around to see who they were, and if the girl would tell them what had happened.

"Whoever killed Enoch doesn't know these woods like we do. We'll find him," Zeb declared.

The girl entered the center of town near the fire, crying and screaming. The men froze in place as she screamed that an orange man had forcefully used her man pleaser. That is what the women in the clan called their vaginas. There was only one woman who came close to identifying it correctly, and she called it her virginia.

The young girl was asked what she meant by orange man, and she described his prison jumper. A few more men from the cabins joined them. All were holding their rifles.

The men starting cranking their flashlights and pointing them outward towards the dark woods.

Her man pleaser? He almost laughed out loud. These country bumpkins were the stereotypical mountain folk he had always heard about, but he didn't believe they existed.

He began to back away just as he heard one of the men say, "Let's git the beast to help."

He had seen the sad, droopy looking hound dog. Doubting they would name that pathetic looking dog the beast, he wondered to what they were referring.

Not having time to stick around, he quietly tried to put as much distance between the hillbillies and himself as he possibly could.

After going fifty yards, he looked back. Illuminated by the fire, he saw the guy who seemed to be the head hillbilly hit the side of a tree with a thick branch. A second after each time that he made connection with the tree trunk, 478923-2021 actually heard it, proving that light traveled faster than sound. It was something he had never experienced first-hand and found that he was amazed by the effect.

He could see others around the fire and the long shadows they cast. He had second thoughts about letting the girl live. He saw her standing by the leader who was still holding the heavy stick.

Raising the rifle to his shoulder, he took aim. 478923-2021 had no idea how straight the sights were on his weapon. He aimed for center mass and squeezed the trigger. The girl fell forward and hit the ground. The sound of his rifle reached the men a second later.

They scrambled for cover. The escaped prisoner laughed and continued on his way, in the dark.

He had no clue where he was going, but as long as it was away from the police, he was happy. He had a rifle and ammo. Even if he would get lost, he would survive.

He kept moving. After a few hours, he began having an unexplainable feeling of danger. He stopped and listened.

He recognized the distant banging of a thick stick against a tree trunk. The hillbillies were still making that noise, but to what end, he was unsure.

478923-2021 saw a distant fire.

Trailhead 3

Cameron Stattlinger sat by the fire, enjoying the light and not really needing the heat for warmth. The temperature was above sixty and very comfortable.

Cam boiled water for a cup of coffee. He should have been asleep, but he just couldn't settle in. He was exhausted from hiking almost thirty miles. Sleep should have come easily. He had no explanation as to why it wasn't.

When his water was ready, he used a coffee bag, similar to a tea bag. He added sugar and dry creamer. He took the first sip and sighed a content little sigh, as the butt of the rifle hit the back of his head.

478923-2021 pulled the pants up, and they fit almost perfectly. The short-sleeved shirt was the same. He rifled through the hiker's backpack and found freeze dried food and trail mix. *I've hit the jackpot*, he thought, as he packed the items back into the pack.

He heard his victim moan. He had him tied up with orange strips from his prison jumper. The same was used as a gag.

A question weighed on his mind and he said it aloud, "Now, should I kill you or let you live?"

The bound hiker's eyes became large as he heard the words. His fate was about to be decided by a total stranger. He struggled with his bindings, but to no avail.

The escaped prisoner thought about the fact that he had killed three human beings in a little over twelve hours: the guard, the hillbilly hunter and the girl. At least he assumed the girl was dead. Three murders and a rape. *I've had quite an impressive day's work*, he thought.

"Don't worry. I'm going to let you live. Killing you wouldn't really serve a purpose. It wouldn't be fun or sporting," he explained to his captive.

That news did nothing to relieve Cameron's anxiety.

The distant rapping sound of a branch against a tree trunk could still be heard sporadically. It was beginning to work on 478923-2021's nerves. *Why are they doing that?* he wondered.

Light was creeping into the realm of darkness. The blackness was retreating and giving way to a world of gray.

The fugitive could make out that he was on a trail. The Trail. The Appalachian Trail.

He was now dressed as a hiker. The trail would lead him to civilization. If he could eventually make his way to Carlisle, he would be home free.

"Hey, how far is it to Carlisle?" he asked.

Cameron didn't answer. He couldn't with the gag in his mouth.

478923-2021 pulled down the gag and said, "Answer me."

"Almost seventy miles," Cameron said. "Just head northeast on this trail."

"Oh, shit! Now you know where I'm headed," 478923-2021 said with the hint of a smile.

"Mister, I won't tell anyone a thing. I promise!" Cameron pleaded.

"Nope. Gotta take chance out of the equation," 478923-2021 said. He grabbed his rifle, placed it against Cameron's head and pulled the trigger. Victim number four.

"I was really hoping to let you live. This is getting to be a habit," he chuckled to himself and the corpse of Cameron Stattlinger.

"I'm hungry."

He began heating some of Cameron's water over the fire. He removed a packet of the freeze-dried beef stroganoff from the backpack.

Twenty minutes later, he was using Cameron's mess kit and eating better than he had in months. At least that was his opinion. In his mind, it was an indictment against prison food that a hiker's freeze-dried meal could taste so good by comparison.

Thwok!

The rapping on the trees was getting closer.

He put out the fire, packed everything into his new backpack and then dragged Cameron's dead body several dozen feet into the underbrush. He placed his orange jumper under the body so it wasn't visible from the trail.

He looked around and everything appeared normal. Once satisfied, he began walking northwards.

Thwok!

"Damn hillbillies are coming for me! The cops are after me. I am one popular man. Carlisle, Pennsylvania, here I come!" he said aloud.

He had a female cousin in Carlisle. He hadn't seen her in years, but that didn't matter. She was family, and he needed somewhere to be headed towards. Otherwise, he was a desperate man adrift in a hostile world. He fixated on reaching his cousin. From there, he had no clue what he would do.

He began hiking. Cameron's hiking boots were a bit small and were starting to hurt his feet.

He wondered why people found this to be enjoyable. Walking in the woods for a few minutes is one thing, but walking hundreds of miles, just to say you did it, was insane.

He heard voices. He peered ahead and could see cops. Four of them. He panicked.

Not knowing what to do, he left the trail and headed towards what he thought was the thickest grouping of trees in the area. He reached the thick trunked behemoths and removed the blue backpack. He sat on it with his back against a tree trunk and waited for the cops to move on.

He held his rifle, but hoped he wouldn't have to shoot it out with them. When he had seen the group of cops, at least two of them had AR15s. He would have loved to have one of those himself.

478923-2021 could hear the four cops talking. They sure weren't worried about stealth. These cops were loud and laughing like they were on a holiday or something.

They passed by and let out a breath that he didn't even know he was holding. Then he sighed.

The cops were walking south, and he was headed north. That was a good piece of luck. He scrambled from out behind of the trees, put the backpack on once again and rejoined the trail.

Thirty minutes later, he could begin to feel the heat of the summer day. It was going to be a scorcher, if he could feel it already in the shade of the forest.

Thwok!

Unbelievable, he thought, *those damn hillbillies just won't stop!* He picked up his pace.

Zeb and his men were moving rapidly. Their rapping call had been answered. The beast was on the move and in the hunt.

The men were furious that their friend had been killed, but even more so over the little girl named Hannah. She died on the ground where she fell. She was the daughter of Ananias McNary, and he was pissed to high heaven, as he put it.

If the hillbillies found 478923-2021 before the cops, he would not be a happy man. And if the beast found him first, his death would be excruciating.

The sun continued to make its lazy arc over the forest. By 11:00 a.m. the temperature had hit eighty-three degrees. The humidity was at a cloying ninety-two percent.

The escaped prisoner was correct. It was going to be a scorcher. Misery was coming, no matter how you looked at it.

Trailhead 4

By 1:00 p.m. the temperature had climbed to ninety degrees. 478923-2021 was sweating heavily. His back was soaked in sweat from the backpack.

"How in the hell do these damn hiking freaks do this? This is madness. Why in the hell would somebody want to hike the Appalachian Trail?" he said aloud, disgusted at any human that would find this to be suitable recreation.

Thwok!

He stopped and looked around. That sounded close.

These hillbilly shitheads never give up, he thought. He left the trail and hid, to see if the hillbillies would show themselves. If they did, he would pick them off, one by one.

What he saw next made his jaw drop.

It responded to the trunk banging. The sasquatch had encountered Zeb's clan years ago. It had been wounded by a large cougar.

The mountain lion did not survive, but it had inflicted a great deal of damage. Zeb, and two others of his clan, had come across the wounded behemoth while hunting.

Severely weakened by the encounter, the sasquatch remained docile while Zeb and his men applied poultices and tried to bandage its wounds. The men also brought it food.

As to why Zeb and his clan would help the creature remained a mystery to most, except Zeb and the other two men. Zeb was a calculating man. He was counting on the beast being grateful.

The McNary's knew of the sasquatch's existence for over one hundred years. It was a live and let live relationship.

The humans knew the beasts were another version of themselves. Zeb had heard talk of something called evolution, back when he worked in Mount Holly Springs.

His understanding was that big monkeys became men. He just didn't understand why there were still big monkeys walking through the forests. He figured once the monkeys changed, they would all change.

No matter how the evolutionary process worked, Zeb knew it could be advantageous having the furry monster in his hip pocket. Every so often, he would bang on a tree and the monster would come. Zeb would give him a newly killed deer.

The sasquatch would take it, and shortly thereafter, the McNary clan would wake up to a beehive full of honey or one or two dead turkeys. It was the beast returning the favor, and it showed that it knew they were in a symbiotic relationship, of sorts.

The sasquatch had helped the clan thrice, when kidnapped women had escaped. It had an uncanny knack for finding those that Zeb wanted found.

478923-2021 was watching an eight-foot-tall ape, yet it wasn't an ape. It reminded him of that big thing in the Star Wars movies, but this thing had a more human-like face.

It was holding his orange jumper in its left hand, or paw, whichever was most appropriate. It was looking his way.

Just then, seven hillbillies burst onto the trail from the forest. He waited to see if the big thing would attack them. It didn't.

The head bumpkin walked up to it and appeared to be talking. It looked at the man and then looked his way. Suddenly, it broke into a run, straight at 478923-2021.

He raised his rifle and fired. It had no effect. He stood up and began running. The beast was on him in a flash.

It picked him up by the backpack and held him several feet off the ground. He dropped his rifle and slipped out of the backpack's straps.

Hitting the ground, he retrieved the rifle and shot the giant in the leg. It howled in pain and stepped backwards.

478923-2021 took off running into the forest.

Before the beast could react, three of the hillbillies shot at the escaped prisoner but missed. Zeb was livid.

Still holding his thick tree wrapping stick, he swore loudly and ran up to the beast and hit it hard on the upper arm. "Damn, worthless critter!" he screamed.

It was the worst and last mistake Zeb would ever make. The sasquatch grabbed him by his dirty, scrawny neck and slammed him against the nearest tree. The impact cracked his skull, killing him almost instantly.

The other clodhoppers wasted no time in seeing whom the sasquatch would target next. They ran away in the direction they had come.

The giant hominid stood, looking at the place where they made their retreat. Then it looked in the direction of 478923-2021's departure. It seemed to be working on a decision.

It began to move swiftly after the escapee that had worn the orange jumper that it had dropped only moments ago.

The sasquatch was angry.

He was running and trying to ignore how badly his feet hurt in the boots that had belonged to the dead hiker.

The escaped murderer was starting to wish he would run into the police. The monster, that he had now shot twice, had frightened him greatly.

His pea shooter .22 rifle would not provide much protection against something that big and strong. He was sure his efforts had only served to anger it.

He saw a sign that had several cities and towns listed. It said that Carlisle was still sixty-one miles away. It might as well have said five hundred miles.

Not knowing about what happened with the creature and the backwoodsmen, he assumed they would hunt him down relentlessly. His feet couldn't take much more and definitely not sixty plus miles.

After only ten more minutes, he stopped. The man on the run removed the hiking boots. 478923-2021 had an idea. He had pocketed a Swiss knife from his hiker victim.

Using the sharp blade, the desperate man cut away the leather upper across the toe area. That was the part of the boot that was crushing his toes. The bottom of his feet would still be protected and that was what he needed most.

He put the dead man's boots back on his feet and continued running. He was moving northwards and praying to a God he had forsaken long ago that he wasn't being followed. His feet felt the immediate relief of his boot reconstruction efforts.

Up ahead he saw two hikers, a man and a woman. They saw him as well and stopped. He wasn't sure why they knew to be immediately wary of him. Then he realized, most hikers wouldn't be carrying a rifle.

He had no intention of hurting them. He simply wanted their money, food and a backpack to carry it.

They were young. The man's named was Joshua and his girlfriend was Belinda. They gladly handed over their money and belongings.

He was off once again, rather proud of himself for not killing them. His mind had been carrying quite a bit of guilt over the deaths he had caused. The little girl and the small-footed hiker were at the top of his list. They didn't really need to die.

The cops would already be on alert in all the nearby towns, including Carlisle. He could have let the hiker go. He enjoyed killing him and that scared him more than anything. Shooting the little girl from afar was fun too. It was a challenge, and it was meant to show those clodhoppers that he was dangerous. That didn't quite work the way he hoped. It just stirred them up.

Letting the hiking couple live was proof he hadn't become a murderous animal. Wasn't it? He was having these conversations with himself, the whole while fearing for his own life.

Forty minutes farther, he stopped, as he saw the huge beast standing on the trail ahead of him. It was staring at him and breathing heavily.

He raised the rifle. If he could just get a good headshot, maybe he'd get lucky and kill it. As he aimed, the beast moved and threw a rock his way.

Pain exploded in his left knee, and he dropped to the ground. He grabbed at his knee and felt an unusual lump. Something was definitely wrong. The pain was bringing tears to his eyes.

He regained some semblance of thought and looked for the beast. It was standing on the trail once again, staring at him.

478923-2021 was panicked. Should he try to shoot at the giant creature, or would that bring another projectile his way. He couldn't just sit there, wounded.

Using the rifle to aid him, he tried to stand. The pain in his left knee was excruciating, but he stood up. He shifted most of his weight to his right leg.

There they stood, staring at one another. A dangerous beast and a dangerous man in a showdown that 478923-2021 knew he couldn't win.

He yelled, "Come on, you big sack of monkey shit! Finish me!"

The large creature only cocked his head, as if to say, are you nuts, little man?

He raised the rifle and took careful aim. It was very difficult, trying to balance on just one leg.

The beast moved, as before, and threw another rock toward him.

The escapee fired as the rock hit him in the stomach, just below his solar plexus. He toppled backwards, and the rifle flew off to his left. It landed eight feet away from him.

The bullet missed the big animal.

478923-2021 moaned and rubbed his stomach. He lie there, wishing the sasquatch would just finish this. Between the injury to his leg and his stomach, all the fight had left him.

He moved to look down the trail for the beast. There it stood, in the same place as before. It continued the strange vigil, not moving any closer.

The desperate man rolled over onto his sore stomach and took a sniper's position. He aimed and fired.

The bullet hit the beast in the leg. It bellowed loudly and grabbed another rock and threw it. The projectile sailed over him. His prone position had made him less of a target.

He fired again.

This time the bullet hit the target mid-torso. It screamed in pain and began running towards him.

He fired once more, aiming at its legs.

The beast came crashing down as the bullet shattered its right patella (kneecap). Both combatants were on the ground, less than forty feet apart.

The monster stared at him with rage and began slowly dragging itself his way.

He fired at his enemy's head. The animal shrieked.

He fired twice more, and it ceased to move.

478923-2021 watched its rib cage to see if it breathed. He could not discern any movement. Somehow, he had killed this king of the forest with a .22 Winchester Rimfire rifle. It seemed impossible to believe, but he had done it.

Now the problem at hand was how to move his wounded body sixty miles to Carlisle. He tried to get up, but a weight was on his back. The weight became increasingly heavier until he couldn't breathe. He heard his own ribs breaking before he passed out.

A squad of Sheriff's deputies found his crushed body on the trail almost four hours later.

An EMT squad was called in to transport the body. They did an initial examination and reported that it had been crushed to death. It made no sense.

His ribs were broken, his knee was shattered and there was nothing nearby to explain it. There were several spots where blood had been shed, mostly south of the victim's body.

They presumed it was his blood. But as to what had crushed him, they had no clue. There weren't any downed trees nearby, under which he might have been pinned.

A few animal hairs were found on him, but they were chalked up to curious critters checking out the dead body.

Ultimately, the most important factor was that they found their escaped prisoner and murderer of a prison guard. Later, the hiker was acknowledged as another one of his victims. The hillbilly hunter and the young girl's deaths were never reported.

The bad man was dead and that was all that mattered in the world of human affairs. But know this, every king of the forest has a queen.

Made in United States
North Haven, CT
05 April 2022

17954403R00078